Returning Home in Summit County

Summit County Series Book 6

Katherine Karrol

Cover Design by Ideal Book Covers

Background photo by Katherine Karrol

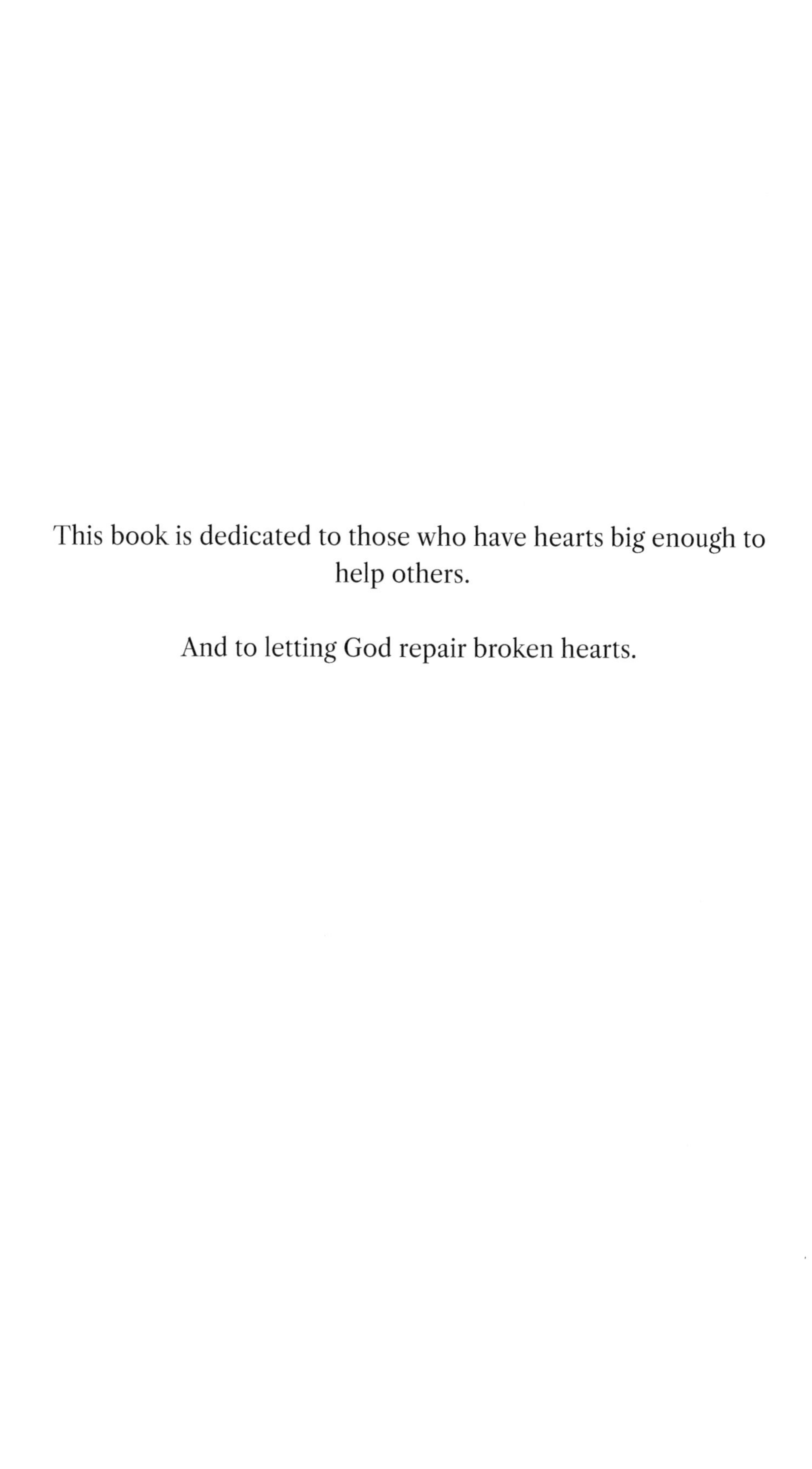

This book is dedicated to those who have hearts big enough to help others.

And to letting God repair broken hearts.

The Summit County Series

The Summit County Series is a group of standalone books that can be read individually, but those who read all of them in order will get a little extra something out of them as they see the characters and stories they've read about previously continue and will get glimpses of characters that may be featured in future books. The series is set in a small county in northern Michigan where everyone knows everyone else, so the same characters and places make cameos and sometimes show up in significant roles in multiple books.

This series is near and dear to the author's heart because her favorite place in the world looks an awful lot like Summit County. She is certain that the people who know her and/or live in the area that inspired Summit County will think characters and situations are based on them or their neighbors (or even on her), and she assures them that they are not. The characters and stories are merely figments of her overly active imagination. Well, except for Jesus. He's totally real.

Chapter 1

THE GIGGLES AND CHEERS of "Mzungu!" from the children fueled Garrett and egged him on. They had loved the Robot, but the Sprinkler put them over the top, as it always did. Even their parents cheered at the laughing white man's strange movements as they all danced together. Just like in every other village, a few brave souls attempted to mimic what he was doing and he took on the task of being their teacher. When he'd learned the dances in fifth grade to make a girl laugh, he had no idea that they would come in so handy years later in a land far away.

The celebration continued into the evening, and the festive atmosphere added to his sense of purpose and accomplishment. Each celebration was different, as each village had its own customs and personality. The one thing they all had in common was the enthusiasm and gratitude of the people.

Building the pumps for the wells was hard work, but it was worth every sore muscle and drop of sweat under the hot African sun. With each one completed, Garrett felt more humbled by the excitement and thankfulness of the people. When he was the age of the children dancing around him, clean water was just one of the many things he took for granted. He was too busy thinking about the next action-hero figures he wanted or the next movie coming out to appreciate the many things he had.

These children, along with their parents, were celebrating and praising God over the clean water that was finally available to them near their own homes. He praised right along with them, for giving them better lives and health and for giving him purpose and a place in the world. Water gave life in more ways than one.

Somehow he heard his own name being called over the laughter and singing. When he looked up, he saw Mukasa, one of the men he traveled and built wells with, running toward him with the satellite phone in his hand. Garrett looked across the way at Isaiah Matembe, his boss and mentor, whose face echoed his own confusion about Garrett being the receiver of a call.

Garrett's heart slammed into his throat. *Laci.*

Mind racing, he sprinted toward Mukasa. A phone call for him on any day that wasn't a holiday could only be bad news.

Please Lord, let her be okay.

There was no one else on earth who knew how to get in touch with him as he traveled through Uganda, so if someone was calling, it was either her or someone calling on her behalf.

He was breathless by the time he put the phone to his ear. "Laci?"

"Garrett!"

Relief at hearing her voice replaced the fear that had gripped him. "Are you okay?"

He could barely hear her through her tears. "It's Dad, Garrett."

Thank God.

"He had a stroke." It was obvious by her voice that she was struggling to speak. "He's paralyzed on one side and can't talk. He's hooked up to a bunch of tubes and . . ."

"I'll get there as soon as I can. Can you take money from my account and book me a flight?"

"You don't have to come, Garrett. I don't know if he'll still be here by the time you can get home."

Home. Not anymore.

"I'm not coming for him, I'm coming for you. Do you have anyone there with you now?"

"I know you can't talk long on that phone, so I'll let you know when I book the flight. Entebbe, right?"

"Right, Entebbe. It's fine, I can talk for a minute. Are you okay?" The one thing he didn't like about living on the other side of the world was not being able to see Laci. He had tried to get her to join him in his mission work, but she felt obligated to stay with Dad.

"I'm okay. I'm just tired." She sniffled on the other end of the line. "Are you sure you want to come?"

No.

"I'm coming. I don't want you to have to do this alone. Book my ticket, and I'll be there."

"Okay. How soon can you get to Entebbe?"

"I can get there within a couple of days, so go ahead and book it. And Laci?"

"Yeah?"

"Make sure you book it round-trip."

Chapter 2

BRIANNA CALLAHAN STRETCHED HER head back and let out a sigh. Her neck and shoulders were in one big knot, and her eyes were dry and blurry. She was using every bit of her willpower to focus. Only two more finals and she would be home free.

As often happened, she hadn't given herself enough time to study the way she wanted to. She was supposed to be done with her job at the VA the day before, but since one of the veterans she had worked closely with had been having a rough time finding low-cost housing, she had spent all afternoon helping him fill out applications and trying to encourage him.

Glancing at her phone, she saw that she was missing a gif war in the ongoing group chat with her two best friends, Shelby Montaugh and Rachel Cooper. It appeared that the theme they'd started was from *Friends*, their favorite old TV show.

She grinned as she scrolled through the gif album in her phone. "Oh, I'm so in this! I need a break anyway." She sent one with Chandler in a bubble bath with a glass of wine in his hand that said, "I've had a very long, hard day." *I know what you mean, Chandler.*

As the videos went back and forth, she laughed so hard that the phone almost slipped out of her hand. It felt good to laugh out loud and be silly after the hectic day she'd had. If someone eavesdropped on their conversations, they might not immediately know that they were three intelligent, responsible women.

Her phone rang and it was a conference call with her fellow gif warriors. "How you doin'?" Her Joey Tribiani impression was pretty good, if she did say so herself.

"Aren't you supposed to be getting ready for a final?" Rachel was always the studious one of the three.

"I needed a break. I've had a very long, hard day too, and it's nowhere near over. My eyes are glazing over, and my brain is oozing out my ears."

"Are you ready for tomorrow?"

"Not even close. I think I'd better hang up and get back to—" The knock at her door startled her, and she wondered who on campus was not cramming. "Someone is at the door. I hope it's Joey's Pizza delivering a deep dish with pepperoni and bacon to the wrong address."

Her foot had fallen asleep from sitting on it, so she hobbled to the door. When she saw the familiar tall frame and boyish features through the window, she gasped.

She whispered into the Bluetooth so that he couldn't hear through the door. "Oh my gosh, it's Corey."

"*What?*" Shelby and Rachel spoke in one voice—one very loud voice.

"Shhh!"

As she considered tiptoeing away from the door and pretending she wasn't home, she realized that he had probably heard her talking before he knocked.

"Keep us on the Bluetooth so we can hear what's going on. We'll hit our mute buttons."

"Rachel, you're so practical. That's a great idea, but nope."

She clicked *End* on the call as she opened the door.

When she saw him standing there with a nervous smile and big bouquet of flowers, her jaw dropped. *Flowers? Really? What's next, a heart-shaped box of chocolates?*

Actually, chocolate sounds good. She peeked to see if he was hiding any somewhere, just in case.

"Hi, Corey. This is a surprise."

When he pulled a large coffee from behind his back, she forgave him for the flowers and lack of chocolate.

"I came to give you a study break." He held out the flowers but she looked instead at the coffee in his hand.

"Is that for me?"

"Two creams and a shot of vanilla, just like you like it." He gave a shy smile as he handed it to her.

She tried to be gracious and to will away her discomfort. "Thank you. What's the occasion?"

"Can I come in? I was hoping that we could chat for a few minutes."

"*Chat*?" Her eyebrows wrinkled in confusion. "Are you done with your finals? Because mine are gonna be a bear. I'm knee-deep in Business Law right now."

He was in the same MBA program she was in and, unlike her, obsessed with his ranking in the class, so there was no way he could be done. She wondered if the pressure of finals got to him and made him lose his once-brilliant mind.

"You need a break. Can I have a few minutes?"

She narrowed her eyes as she considered whether or not she could afford to take the time. His sheepish smile softened her resolve, and she stepped aside to let him in.

He looked around, as if waiting for an invitation to sit. She didn't have time to stroll down memory lane, so she just stood there looking at him and hoping he would get to the reason for his visit.

"Why are you here, Corey? And why are you bringing me flowers?" *And how did you remember my coffee order but not the fact that I think flowers are silly and a waste of money?*

"I wanted to see if we could talk."

She couldn't imagine what they needed to talk about. They had broken up right before Christmas, and apart from friendly greetings in the classes they shared, they hadn't spoken since. "What do you want to talk about?"

"Us."

Oh, come on. It's finals week. I don't have room in my brain for this. "Us? What about us?"

"Well . . . I think we were pretty good together, and I think you were premature in ending our relationship when you did." He took a breath as if trying to inhale courage. "If I walk away from here after graduation and go back to Toledo without at least trying, I'm going to regret it."

She stepped back and took another sip of her coffee, thankful to have something to do with her mouth other than speak while she absorbed what he was saying. He looked so sweet and nervous standing there, and she didn't know how to respond. She didn't want to hurt his feelings, but it was cruel to give people false hope, and she refused to do it. "I don't get this, Corey. We broke up."

"I know, I know, I'm a great guy. It's not me, it's you." He gave her the teasing half-smile that she had always found endearing.

She couldn't help but chuckle at the way he parroted back the words she had used when she ended the relationship before Christmas, and she remembered why she had gone out with him for as long as she did. His sense of humor and kindness had drawn her to him in the first place and kept her with him longer than with almost any other boyfriend.

He looked at her earnestly. "If it's really me, then I want you to be straight and tell me exactly what it was about me that you suddenly found so intolerable. The last conversation we had before the one in which you very gently but firmly dumped me gave me no hint that anything was wrong." He fidgeted with the flowers as he pushed through his speech. "I thought things were great between us. We had fun in Ohio on Thanksgiving and my family loved you. We had plans for Christmas and were talking about you moving to Toledo after graduation, and then you just ended it."

He rubbed his neck as he waited for her to say something. When she just looked at him in stunned silence, he continued. "Regardless of any future we might have, I need to know what actually happened. If it's me, I need you to tell me what I did. And if it's you, I need to know if you've gotten yourself together between then and now. Either way . . . I want another chance."

Chapter 3

GARRETT TRIED TO SHAKE the memories that had tormented him all night. He'd shuddered and twitched as he relived the last argument he had with Dad, the one that almost ended with Garrett throwing his first punch.

It was the end of his junior year in college, and he had needed his passport for a short-term mission trip he was planning to take. While searching through a box in the basement, he found the papers that changed his life.

Dad was sitting in the living room staring at the TV and nursing a beer, as had become his nightly habit, when Garrett stalked into the room with some of the papers clutched in his fist.

"Dad, what is this?"

Dad looked at him with the usual dismissiveness and turned back to the TV.

"I asked you a question. What is this?"

"You tell me, smart guy."

"These are scholarship papers—with my signature that isn't my signature. Why is there a scholarship here that I never knew anything about?"

Garrett shoved the papers in his face, trying to drag his attention from the TV he insisted on parking himself in front of every night.

Dad swatted his hand away. "That was my decision to make. You were seventeen years old."

"Why would you *decide* to lie to me? You hid the fact that there was a scholarship so that you could let me think that you were paying for everything and could call all the shots."

Dad slowly sipped his beer and continued staring at the TV as if he hadn't just been caught in the deception of his life. If he knew that the scholarship papers weren't the only ones Garrett had found, he wouldn't be so nonchalant. Garrett wasn't sharing the other financial papers he had found in that box just yet.

"All these years you let me think you were paying for my college. You made me agree to something that ruined my life in order to get my college education and held this money over my head all this time. It was all a lie." Garrett could see the heat rising in Dad's face even as he continued to ignore him, but he was too livid to back down. "Why would you do this?"

Dad jerked out of his chair and stood nose to nose with him. "Watch your tone, young man. You have no right to question the decisions I make as your father." Garrett could smell the beer on his breath as he spat his words. "You were too blind to see what was good for you. Did you ever stop to think I was protecting you from your own bad decisions?"

"You weren't protecting me. You were manipulating me."

"I did you a favor."

The slight, brief smile of satisfaction on his face bordered on glee. The consequences of the agreement he had forced Garrett into couldn't be reversed, and he knew he had won.

Garrett had never been a violent person or a hothead. He had never been in a fight in his life, and yet he had never wanted to punch someone as much as he wanted to punch his own father in that moment.

Dad held his ground, daring Garrett with his eyes. "What are you gonna do about it?"

In quite possibly the greatest moment of self-control of his life, Garrett turned away from the taunt and walked toward the door.

He turned and looked at Dad for what he promised himself was the last time. "We're done. Have a nice life."

The porch shook as he slammed the door behind himself. As he stormed down the stairs and toward his car, he swore he would never set foot in that house again.

For six years he'd kept that promise to himself. He had left town, finished his degree early, then left the state and eventually the country. Now he was days away from returning and being face-to-face with the man he never wanted to see again.

Chapter 4

BRIANNA COULDN'T FOCUS. SHE tried to return to studying, but her mind went back to Corey's visit earlier. *Why on earth would he want to start a relationship again? He's a great guy, but if we were that good together, I wouldn't have ended it.*

She had learned that directness was the kindest approach in such matters and that playing games only hurt people. Playing anything was not her style, especially with men. She had also learned the hard way what happened when she was open and vulnerable with them. As much as she believed in those as good things in theory, she stayed far from them in practice.

When the phone rang, it jolted her out of her thoughts and back to reality.

"Shelby, since when do you have the energy to be this impatient?"

"Since I'm getting better." Shelby had been sick for years, but after being diagnosed with Lyme Disease and getting the right treatment, she was finally getting some relief.

Rachel's voice reappeared. "I'm here, too. So? What happened?"

Brianna deadpanned, "We're getting married."

Shelby broke into giggles. "I guess we had that coming. So, what did he have to say?"

"He wants another chance and wants me to move to Ohio to see what happens."

"Please tell me you said no." Rachel's voice was tinged with apprehension.

"I told him I'm too busy figuring out my future to think about romance—after I reminded him that I broke up with him months ago."

"Ouch." Rachel's wince came through the phone line. "Even the second time you don't soft pedal anything."

"Of course I don't. He's a good guy, and it's cruel to string people along."

"Must be rough to have someone pining away for you." It was good to hear Shelby feel well enough to really laugh again.

"You're one to talk." Brianna laughed along with her. "You got the great Clay Cooper to pine away for you and beg you to go out with him. I'd say you're doing pretty well in the romance department too." Clay was Rachel's brother-in-law and had been Shelby's dream man since they were teenagers. He had never noticed her when they were younger, but as of a couple of months ago, he had not only noticed, but pulled out all the stops to pursue her and make her his. He was at least as smitten with her as she was with him.

Brianna could hear the grin in her friend's voice. "He's incredible. Oh, and he's here for our movie-on-the-couch date! Talk to you tomorrow!" *Click.*

"Those two would be sickening if they weren't so adorable." Since Rachel's husband Derek and Clay were brothers, Rachel had a front-row view of the rapidly growing relationship. "Okay, back to you. I want all the details before Derek gets home."

"There aren't really any more details. He's a great guy, but that ship sailed months ago."

Rachel chuckled. "They always do."

"It's true." Brianna sighed. She didn't bother to dispute her history of breaking off relationships as soon as they became serious.

"You did end that pretty abruptly, though, even for you. One minute, he was coming up to spend a week with your family before Christmas and the next—or rather, after a two-minute phone call—you were done with him."

"I know, but I told you when he had to cancel his trip to see me because of the snow, I realized I wasn't the least bit disappointed. Why would I stay in a relationship that doesn't have the power to disappoint me?"

Rachel giggled. "Wow, that's deep."

"Feel free to use it in your next book." In addition to working at the library in Hideaway, Rachel had a side career as an author, and her friends had taken to feeding her lines to use.

"Oh, I'm definitely going to use that. But back to you. You've broken up with more decent guys than most women ever meet, let alone date. I think you have a problem."

Brianna shrugged. "Whatever. Maybe I'm emotionally unavailable, whatever that means."

"I don't think people who are the kind of friend or sister or aunt you are can be emotionally unavailable. You're the best friend Shelby or I could ever ask for, and not one of your family members would trade you for anything."

"Thanks, Rach."

"Maybe you're just romantically challenged. You have big, thick walls built around your heart when it comes to men."

And I remember exactly when the first brick was put into place.

Chapter 5

As the car came to a halt in front of the Entebbe airport, Garrett felt his chest clench. He stared at the hills in the distance, trying to memorize the view, just as he had when they passed Lake Victoria.

Isaiah sat quietly for a moment before interrupting. "Are you ready for your next journey?"

"Honestly? No." He looked out at the travelers bustling around the entrance without seeing any of them. "Hopefully by the time I land, I will be. I've got thirty-six hours and four flights to do so, not counting the hours I'll be here waiting."

"The Lord will do His work in you, my son. He will go before you and walk beside you." The man's bright smile could light up a dark sky but was powerless against Garrett's mood.

"I know He will. We'll spend a lot of time together getting my head ready on the flights." Garrett tried to force a reassuring smile at him.

He hated leaving Isaiah as much as he hated leaving Africa. In the three short years since they had met, Isaiah had become a father figure and had taught him more about what it meant to love others and live for Christ than all the years of Sunday School and youth groups combined.

Isaiah met him at the side of the car. "I know you're planning to come back, but in case you don't, take this." He pressed an envelope with what looked like a long letter into his hand.

"I'm coming back." Garrett spoke with more confidence than he felt. "This is my home, and I've got my return ticket for six weeks from now."

"My son, you don't know what the Lord has planned for you in your homeland. He has grown you here and has used you mightily. Even if your time here is finished, your service is not." He grabbed Garrett and gave him a bear hug. "I pray that I will see you again this side of heaven, but more than that, I pray for God's will for you. I believe He has work for you in your village."

Garrett didn't want to consider the possibility of not returning, but he knew the man was right. This might be goodbye. "Thank you for everything, Isaiah. You saved my life when you found me in Queensland. God brought you into my life to turn it around, and even if He interrupts my plans to come back here, I won't forget you."

Isaiah chuckled. "You were a lost and wandering boy when the Lord brought us together on that beach, but He had His sights on you and turned you into a man. I only obeyed Him." He placed his hands on Garrett's shoulders as he looked into his eyes. "He used you to give me life, too, and used us to give my people life through the pumps. He will continue His work through us, and we will meet again."

Isaiah turned and walked back to his side of the car. As he waved and smiled, Garrett felt as if his feet were made of cement.

Africa was home now. Michigan seemed like another world, or at least another lifetime. He had spent so much time trying to forget it, and especially to forget some of the memories there, that it felt as if he was about to get on a plane to go to a new land. *Lord, please let me come back here, to my real home. And please let it be soon.*

He held tightly to the bag that contained all of his worldly possessions as he watched Isaiah's car shrink in the distance and the busy travelers passed by him on all sides. Turning to face the main entrance to the airport, he took a deep breath and started walking.

It was no surprise to receive extra scrutiny, being a young man traveling alone internationally with only a backpack and a small duffel bag, so he tried to exercise patience as he answered the same questions over and over.

"Yes, I am an American."

"Yes, I live in Uganda."

"I'm going to America for a family emergency."

"No, I don't have any more luggage."

"I'm coming back."

When he got to his gate, he stared out the window at the place he didn't want to leave. He used to enjoy people-watching in airports, but today was different. With the heaviness he was feeling, he didn't want to see the excited faces of young lovers on their way to exotic destinations, the weary ones of mothers trying to wrangle their children, or the focused ones of business travelers trying to get home to their families.

His own trip was neither business nor pleasure, neither anticipated vacation nor tedious business trip. His was purely out of obligation.

Unlike his fellow travelers, he was on his way to the place he had tried to get as far away as possible from, and he was going to face the man he had hoped to never see again. If he could, he would trade places with any one of the people around him.

While he waited, he replayed the phone call from Laci. The disappointment in her voice when he had said he wanted a round-trip ticket had sent a wave of guilt through him. Hurting her was never something he could stomach, and if he could avoid it, he would.

After their call had ended, his first thought was that the act of vengeance God had been saving up for Dad for the way he had lived his life and treated people had finally come to pass. He knew that wasn't how God did things, but for the man who always said he would rather die by a bullet to the back than have any kind of physical weakness, surviving a stroke and being dependent on other people was the ultimate punishment.

Garrett took no delight in thinking that he got what he deserved. Over time the hatred he'd once had toward him had turned to pity, and he didn't have ill will toward him or wish bad things upon him. Dad's current suffering wouldn't remove all the damage that he had inflicted long ago. It wouldn't bring Mom back or help Laci or bring back all that Garrett had lost.

As he got settled into his seat on the plane, he pulled out his Bible and started reading, knowing that it would serve a dual purpose. It would be good to be reminded both of how God expected him to behave toward Dad and of how faithful He was, even—or maybe especially—in the most difficult circumstances. It would also discourage fellow travelers from starting conversations with him on the flight. He had found out by accident many years ago that nobody wanted to talk to the person on the plane who was reading the Bible. It was a sad statement, but he wasn't one to look a gift horse in the mouth, and it was serving his goal of avoiding small talk and preparing to return to Michigan quite well.

He had to turn away from the window as the plane ascended and his home for the last three years disappeared from view. *This is not goodbye.*

Chapter 6

BRIANNA WAS ONE STEP closer to freedom. Also terror. There was nothing she hated more than uncertainty, and come graduation day, she had no idea what she was going to do.

As she walked through the University of Michigan campus for one of the last times as a graduate student, she forced her attention from the anxiety that was creeping into her mind to the beautiful, old buildings that she would miss seeing every day. Any time the weather and her schedule cooperated, she took a circuitous route by the union and through the law quad where she gazed in awe over the gothic architecture.

Even though she was almost to her least favorite part of the walk, referred to as Hippie Haven by her friends and Body Odor Alley by her, she was taking in the sights. She saved taking in the smells for other parts of campus; all the patchouli oil in the world couldn't cover up the stench left by soap deficiency. Fortunately, when she returned to Hideaway, her tiny hometown in Northern Michigan, in a few days, she would be surrounded by people who appreciated a good shower now and then.

Her Bluetooth trilled in her ear, and she grinned when a glance at the phone showed her it was Rachel.

"Hi, Rach!"

"I'm here, too!" Shelby was obviously next to Rachel and sharing the speakerphone. Between conference calls when they were all at different colleges and speakerphones when two were together and one was away, technology had been a great help to their long friendship.

"Are you done with your Hostile Takeover final?" Shelby giggled even more than usual when she was coming up with her own names for Brianna's classes.

"All done. Only one more presentation to go, thank God. I'm on my way home now."

"You're walking through BO Alley, aren't you? I can hear you trying not to breathe." Rachel had always been the perceptive one. No one picked up on a change in voice or facial expression the way she did.

Brianna tried to speak while letting out as little air as possible. "Trying."

"You can do it! Walk faster!" Shelby sounded more like a cheerleader than the athlete she used to be. Even when she didn't feel well, she was bubbly and upbeat. Now that she and Clay were together, her up went even higher.

"I think I can, I think I can . . ." She picked up her pace after getting a fresh whiff of a guy who was anything but fresh.

"Focus on us. We'll get you through. Shelby and I wanted to call you to plan for a special girls' lunch to celebrate when you get back."

"We know you'll be busy with wedding errands, but we want to be able to give you a proper celebration."

"I would love that!" She grinned into the phone at her sweet friends. "I promised Joe I would be on auntie duty as much as he needs me, but I can work around that."

Her brother Joe was just over a week away from getting married, and Brianna had told him he had first dibs on her time as the day approached. He was a widower and, along with their sister Claire, Brianna had always taken on as much of a substitute mother role as she could with his three-year-old daughter, Lily. Now that Lily was about to have a full-time mother, Brianna wanted to soak up any time she could have with her.

Shelby sounded like she wouldn't take no for an answer. "You can bring Lily if you need to. Rachel is afraid time is going to get away from us and you're going to find a job or take Corey up on his offer and move."

"I have no idea what I'm going to do job-wise and have no intention of moving away from Hideaway, so don't rent a moving truck just yet. For now, all I can think of is my last presentation tomorrow."

She took a deep breath once she turned a corner and got away from the shower haters. "Pray for me tonight. I just need to get through one more class and I'm done with school."

Shelby chuckled. "That's what you said last time you got a college degree."

"Ugh, I need you two to stop me if I ever say I'm going back to school again."

She thought she was done when she got her bachelor's degree in Social Work four years ago, but after a frustrating stint working for the state, she went back for her MBA so that she could gain some skills, tools, and contacts to prepare the way to make a difference in the world. "Tell me again why I thought it was a good idea to get an MBA."

Rachel was quick to answer. "Something about the system being a total disaster and you needing to infiltrate it, blow it up, and rebuild it correctly."

Shelby chimed in, too. "And save the world!"

The reminder that she had no idea how she was going to make a difference in the world brought a knot to her stomach. She would need to think about that later, after her tests were over.

"Thanks for walking me home, you guys. Your timing was perfect. Now I need to go in and hit the books again."

As she was digging her keys out of her bag, a sudden silence filled the other end of the phone. Brianna glanced at her screen to make sure she hadn't accidentally hung up. Silence was not generally a part of any conversation between the three of them, so something was up. "Okay, what's going on?"

Shelby sounded hesitant. "There's something we need to tell you."

"Okayyyy . . . ." Brianna waited for someone to say something, and she pictured them motioning each other to say whatever it was. "Helloooo! Do rock-paper-scissors or something and spit it out. What's going on?"

When Rachel grunted, Brianna knew Shelby had won.

"You know you can just tell me. I'm the direct one, remember? I can take bad news as well as I can dish it out. What's got you two so silent?" She knew it wasn't serious news about a loved one, because they would have told her right away. This had to be more annoyance than emergency.

"Okay. We don't want you to stress, but we want you to be warned."

"Got it. Not stressed, just warned. Go ahead—rip the bandage off fast." She couldn't imagine what it was they were holding out on telling her and tried not to get impatient as she set her bag on the table and headed to the kitchen to make lunch.

"Well, we heard something today . . . about Garrett."

Brianna froze with her hand on the refrigerator door.

Determined not to react to any rumors about him, she tried to act nonchalant. "What did you hear?"

"He's coming home."

"*What?*"

No! No, no, no!

Shelby spoke softly. "Are you okay? We wanted to warn you so you won't be blindsided if you run into him somewhere."

Brianna felt like her brain had just gotten tossed into a Cuisinart and her thoughts were spinning in ten different directions at turbo speed. "Why would he come back? Did Surfers without Borders close down?"

Silence again.

"Who did you hear this from, anyway?" After grabbing sandwich supplies and grapes, she closed the refrigerator door more forcefully than intended.

Shelby hesitated before answering. "I ran into Laci this morning at the store."

Brianna's heart sank. If anyone would know his whereabouts and schedule, it would be his younger sister.

"So much for it being a rumor then."

"Their dad had a stroke."

Couldn't have happened to a nicer guy. Her stomach immediately clenched with guilt. *I'm sorry, Lord.*

"How bad is he?"

Shelby spoke calmly. "It sounds pretty bad. Laci looked exhausted, and she's really worried. She's been afraid Garrett wouldn't get here in time."

"People that mean don't die." Thankfully, her friends knew her better than anyone and knew she wasn't as heartless as she may have sounded upon hearing the news that someone was hovering near death. "I'll be praying for him, I promise. Even mean people need prayer. And if anyone can cheat death, it's him."

Lord, please help. I can't have Garrett Ryan in my head today.

"Pray for Laci, too. She's having a hard time."

"Of course." That would be the easy prayer. "I'm glad she'll have help."

I need to get out of this conversation. "I really need to go, you guys. I can't think about Gar—about other stuff right now. I'm already at my limit with the presentation that I need to be ready for at eight in the morning, and I don't have extra room in my brain."

"Are you going to be okay?" Shelby's voice was full of concern.

"Sure. I haven't seen him in years, and I'll just—I probably won't even recognize him if I see him. It will be fine."

It will be fine.

She stared at the notecards piled on her coffee table and tried to switch gears in her head. "Okay, I really need to go now. Pray for me so I can focus, and I'll talk to you tomorrow."

"Okay, love you!"

"Love you too!"

She set her plate on the coffee table and flopped onto the couch.

Garrett.

After fighting a losing battle with a stream of memories in her head, she focused on pulling herself together. Sitting up and bowing her head over clasped hands, she followed through on the promise she had made to her friends.

"Lord, please be with Mr. Ryan. I don't know how to pray for him, but You know what he needs, and You numbered his days before he was born. If it is Your will, please heal him. Above all, remind him who You are. He loved You once, and he needs You just like the rest of us. Maybe more." She swallowed as she willed herself to say the name she wanted to forget. "Please be with Garrett and Laci. Please be their comfort and give them wisdom if they have to make hard decisions together. And please help me to focus on what I need to do this afternoon. I need to be getting ready for an exam, not thinking about jerks who shattered my heart into a thousand pieces."

Chapter 7

GARRETT RUBBED HIS EYES and thanked the stewardess for the hot coffee that he hoped would help him become alert enough to get off the plane and to his last gate. Thankfully, he'd had an easy time sleeping on the fourteen-hour flight from Doha to Chicago. After sleeping on thin floor mats, airplane seats weren't bad. He planned to take full advantage of the hour layover in Chicago by spending a little bit of time walking through the airport and stretching his legs while he made his way to his next gate for the flight to Traverse City.

As the plane descended over Chicago toward O'Hare, he looked out the window. He had never been a fan of big cities, but after spending three years living in open spaces and small villages, it sickened him to see the unnatural sight of skyscrapers and freeways. *How do people live like this?*

He tried to stretch to look out the window on the opposite side of the plane, where at least he could catch a glimpse of Lake Michigan, but the woman in the window seat apparently preferred the beige shade to the beautiful blue water outside.

Garrett felt like a stranger in a strange land when he walked off the plane and into the airport. It had been four years since he had been on U.S. soil and zero since he'd missed it. As he splashed cold water on his face in the bathroom, he looked into the mirror. In Africa, his white *mzungu* skin stood out to the point that most of the children wanted to touch it, but he felt like he fit there. In Chicago, he looked like many other men walking through the airport but couldn't possibly have felt more out of place.

Even though he had to dodge throngs of people while he meandered toward his gate, it was good to walk after the long flight. He kept his eyes focused on the gate numbers so that he didn't pass his. When he found it and saw that they weren't anywhere near boarding, he walked further down the concourse to give his legs some more exercise before sitting in yet another cramped seat. At least the flight to Traverse City would be short.

He chided himself for being thankful that he hadn't had to make small talk on the long flight. It was good to read, pray, and sleep as he prepared for his return to the place that was once home. He didn't remember the last time he had gone that long without talking to another human being, especially while sitting next to one, but he needed the solitude the Bible and language barrier gave him. Laci would be waiting, and they had plenty to talk about, so maybe it was good that his mouth and ears got to rest up before seeing her.

His mind drifted to some of the other people in town he was looking forward to seeing now that he was going back to Hideaway. He had left a lot of people behind when he left town six years ago. There were some old friends he was hoping to see, but since he had cut off contact with everyone in Hideaway when he left, he wasn't so sure anyone would want to see him. He wished he could skip the visit with Dad and go right to see the others; he had some making up to do and was hoping to do it as soon as possible.

Brianna's face kept getting in the way of the ones he wanted to see, and he tried to shove it from his mind. Again. *Lord, hers is the last face I want in my mind. I haven't even tried to forget Dad the way I've tried to forget her. And now here I am, making my way to a gate and a plane that are going to take me back to both of them.*

Please help me forget.

He rubbed his eyes again, trying to clear a memory of her grin as she leaned in to kiss him.

Walking through the airport was a surreal experience as he looked at the people sitting next to outlets charging multiple mobile devices and looking at those devices instead of speaking to their traveling companions. He noticed a family consisting of a mother, father, and two children and felt a wave of sadness when he looked at them. They each had their own device with matching headphones and bags from Disney.

Wow. They're on their way back from the happiest place on earth and no one is talking about their trip or even looking at souvenirs.

His childhood would have been much easier if there would have been access to all those devices and headphones. If his family would have all been connected to them, maybe Dad would have had less influence on their moods as they traveled—actually as they did anything.

He couldn't tear his eyes away from the family. The boy and girl looked like they had the same age difference as himself and Laci, three years. When his family traveled, he and Laci had played games with each other, and Mom had extended their vacations by reminiscing about every detail with them and listening to every story they told as if it were the first time. Those kids had no idea what they were missing out on by not rehashing their trip with their mom. It would have been nice to have his own father connected to some headphones and his eyes glued to a screen throughout their childhoods so that he wouldn't be chastising and criticizing them for everything they did.

With what those kids were missing with their father, he wondered if his own experience was a gain or if it came out even. Quickly, he knew the answer. He wouldn't have exchanged the time he had with Mom for anything in the world.

It felt like the airport went silent and air became thin when he realized that the father that he was going to visit was as uncommunicative as the father he was now staring at. The only difference was that instead of being engrossed in something on a device in the palm of his hand, his own father was unable to communicate because a stroke had stolen his abilities.

He tried to picture what he would look like in the bed as a way to prepare himself. In their brief phone calls, all Laci had said was that he was paralyzed on his left side, couldn't speak, and was hooked up to a lot of tubes. Garrett couldn't help but wonder if he still had the ability to stare disapprovingly. He would find out soon enough.

The squawk of the overhead announcement startled him, and it felt as if someone had just thrown cold water on his face. "Flight 4067 to Traverse City is now boarding."

Chapter 8

BRIANNA LAUGHED ALONG WITH the others from her Business Law class as they mimicked the mannerisms and rehashed the stories of their professor. He was definitely the most "interesting" professor any of them had ever had. They were all convinced that he practiced his stories in front of a mirror, complete with facial expressions and gestures.

When the stories ended and conversation turned to their futures, Brianna started planning her exit. She was one of only two in the group who didn't have a six-figure corporate job waiting, and the other one who didn't was forming a startup with venture capital funds he'd already secured.

It wasn't that she hadn't had offers. One didn't attain an MBA from the University of Michigan without being courted by a slew of corporations and consulting firms. Her problem was that all of the job offers were the opposite of what she wanted to do. The idea of spending most of her life in boardrooms and climbing corporate ladders sounded like a nightmare to her. She would be blazing her own path, as soon as she figured out what the destination was.

She had gotten her degree so that she would be in a position to help people who were forgotten by society or were struggling to make something of themselves. Her work with the state after she got her undergrad degree had been an exercise in futility and frustration, and she felt like it was doling out much-needed water to thirsty people drip by drip. She had applied to grad school with dreams of either reforming the system or creating something else that would do what she thought the existing system was failing so miserably at. By the time she entered the classroom, she decided that creating something to make the old systems obsolete would be easier than trying to reform them.

As she got up to pretend to go to the bathroom and make her getaway, she saw Corey walk in with some friends. She was still not ready to continue the conversation they had started a few nights ago and didn't want to make it awkward for either herself or him. Pretending to look for something in her purse, she kept her head low as she cut through the kitchen and out the door.

She drove slowly, savoring her last evening as a resident of Ann Arbor and saying goodbye to all the places where she had made so many fond memories. There were a lot of things she would miss about the town, even though she was looking forward to getting home.

Her excitement about returning home had been dampened when she found out that Garrett was going there too. Avoiding people in a small town was a big challenge, and it infuriated her to think about having to be on the lookout for him as she went about her days. She had cut off the conversation about him with Rachel and Shelby before getting to the detail of whether he was coming for a visit or for good, and she shivered when she thought of the possibility that he might be home to stay.

It had been convenient through the years since they had broken up that he was off surfing the globe and living the life of a nomad. Brianna hadn't had to think about seeing him, let alone actually be in the same room with him, for so long that it had almost become natural for him to not be a part of her life. She had refused to let her friends or family bring up his name or give her any updates about him, so she didn't know anything about him anymore.

The last she had heard was that he was in Australia living on a beach, surfing and squandering his life away. Now that they would be sharing the same small town again, there was a very real possibility that she would be forced to be around him.

She shook the thought from her mind. "He doesn't exist anymore. He's a non-entity. Get him out of your brain."

Chapter 9

GARRETT DIDN'T KNOW WHY he felt so tense as he walked off the plane in Traverse City. He was nervous about seeing Dad in a hospital bed, but it wasn't like the man had any power over him anymore. He didn't even have power over himself at the moment, so Garrett didn't need to prepare to respond to any attempts at manipulation or control. The only viable threat was memories.

When he caught a glimpse of Laci through the sparse crowd outside security, she was like a gust of fresh air. She was jumping up and down in her excitement, her blonde curls bouncing right along with her.

"Garrett!" She squealed as he passed the security gate.

"Laci Lou!" He dropped his bag on the floor as he swooped her up into a hug and twirled her around. In that moment, there was a part of him that felt good being home.

He ignored that part.

It was only when he released her that he saw the dark circles under her eyes, and seeing that made him glad that he'd made the trip. Spending her days in the hospital room was taking its toll on her, and he hoped to lighten the load she had been carrying. He wished he hadn't committed to going straight to the hospital from the airport, but the sooner he could get it over with, the better.

They walked out into the evening, and it felt good to breathe fresh air again after spending the past forty hours in airports and on planes.

"Do you remember how to drive?"

He held out his hand for her keys and snickered. "Better than you."

"Hey!" She playfully smacked him on the arm.

"I'm not the one who got in an accident on their nineteenth birthday."

"It was freezing rain, Garrett. The cop didn't even ask questions about it . . . *because it was freezing rain.* My driving record has been perfectly spotless since then." They laughed together as she tried to grab the keys back, and he tousled her hair and pushed her toward the passenger side door.

As they started on their way, Garrett knew he couldn't avoid the topic of the hour any longer. "So . . . what do I need to know before I see Dad?"

Her face fell. "He's in really bad shape, Garrett. I wasn't sure if he would still be here by the time you got home."

Home. There was that word again.

"I've been trying to picture in my mind what he'll look like so I'm more prepared."

"You won't even recognize him." Her eyes had a haunted look, and he realized he'd greatly underestimated the toll it was taking on her. "He looks like he's aged twenty years in the week since this happened."

Garrett reached over and grasped her hand. "I'm sorry for making it harder by asking about it."

"Having you here is making it easier. I'm sorry that you had to come home for this, but I'm so thankful to have you here." She smiled at him as she wiped the tears that had escaped her eyes.

The drive to the hospital only took ten minutes, and Garrett prayed silently as he drove that there would be peace and healing for his family during his six-week visit. He had no idea what that could look like, but he had learned over time that he could ask God for big things and that God could deliver them.

It felt like his lungs shrunk as he turned onto the street that led to the hospital. When he noticed that Laci was staring at him, he looked over at her. "What?"

"Nothing." She looked back at the road ahead.

When he shifted his own eyes back to the road, he noticed the speedometer and saw that he was driving five miles per hour. *Oh.*

He turned back to her with a sheepish smile. "I guess I'm not in a hurry to walk in there and see this."

She put her hand on his and squeezed it. "It's okay. We're walking in together."

When they walked into the hospital room, Garrett gasped. The mental preparation he had attempted fell short.

The weak man in the bed looked nothing like the one Garrett had been intimidated and controlled by his whole life. He looked back at the name on the wall to confirm that it was, in fact, Dad. As Laci had warned, he did look like he'd aged twenty years, at least. He looked like a small, weak shell of the man Garrett remembered. The pity he had been feeling for his father's isolated existence only grew. It didn't matter that he had created it by his own behavior.

Garrett looked around the room. There were no get well cards, nor was there any evidence that anyone had been to see him other than Laci. The relationships he had damaged in the years after his wife died hadn't ended with his children.

The nurse on duty gestured to them to meet her in the hallway. When he stepped out of the room, he felt like he could breathe again.

He tried to focus on the words she was saying, but all he heard were random syllables. Laci was nodding along and seemed to understand what she said and what it all meant. When his stomach growled, Laci looked up at the clock and suggested they get something to eat and head to Dad's house for a good night of sleep so they could come back in the morning.

As they walked out, he turned to her. "Is that what it's like all day every day?"

"Yeah."

"Well, if you need a break from all of this, I can come alone tomorrow."

She had tears in her eyes when she looked up at him. "I have to be here."

"Okay. We'll be here together."

Garrett forced himself to use a casual tone when he asked about Laci's boyfriend of two years. "I haven't heard you mention Ronnie. Has he been here with you at all?" There was nothing about him or that relationship that Garrett thought was good for her.

"No, he's been really busy." She looked away. "He's come over to see me a couple of times when I've gone home at night."

I'll bet he has. Thinking about how far the guy had probably tried to push the relationship made Garrett sick to his stomach. He hoped that a free meal was all he was getting on those late night visits. Laci deserved to have someone in her life who would treat her with respect and dignity and who would be at her side supporting her, but he knew Ronnie was not that guy.

"He hasn't been here with you at all this past week?" Garrett didn't want to put her into the position of defending the greaseball, but he couldn't help himself.

She looked down, and her tone reflected her disappointment. "He's really busy."

"Okay." The rest of that conversation was going to have to wait, and he was too tired to know how to approach it in a way that would get Laci to open up.

Chapter 10

Graduation Day. After two years of hard work, laser focus, and late nights, it's finally here. And I am really done with school this time.

Brianna chuckled as she shoved the last suitcase into the back seat of her car, which was piled high with pretty much everything she owned. When she drove by the arena where the ceremony was taking place, she waved and smiled at the students and families milling about outside.

"Buh-bye fellow graduates! Sorry to miss the three hours of boring—oops, I mean inspirational—speeches and the ten seconds of hearing your name and walking across the stage. You all have a great time. I'm going home!"

There was no point in attending the graduation ceremonies. Sitting there enduring a bunch of long speeches telling graduates how accomplished they were and what great things they were going to do in the business world sounded like as much fun as chewing glass. She also didn't feel like spending any more time talking with her fellow graduates about all the grand plans they had after graduation when she herself was, for the first time in her life, feeling completely directionless. After her surprise visit from

Corey and the close call at the pub, she was even more glad she hadn't gotten tickets to graduation.

It was time to go home and figure out the rest of her life.

As she got on the freeway and headed north toward Hideaway, she tried to focus on the positives that were coming in her immediate future. "Okay, stop feeling sorry for yourself. You're going home, for one. You're going to be able to spend time with everyone you love and won't have to cram everything you want to do into a weekend anymore. The wedding next weekend is going to be great and you're getting an amazing sister-in-law in Emily. Before and after the wedding, you're going to be able to spend tons of time with little Lily. You're even finally going to be able to be involved in-person with the fundraiser for the new treatment center instead of through email and phone calls."

Rachel's parents, Rick and Faith Weston, were starting a new treatment center for pain and addiction in town, and if Shelby was well enough by the time they got it up and running, she would be the Activity Therapist. She was working temporarily as an administrative assistant to Faith, which she was able to do mostly from home. Brianna called her to get an update and a much-needed dose of optimism.

"Brianna! Are you on the road yet?"

"I am! I'm about an hour into the trip."

She could hear Shelby clapping her hands through the phone. "I'm so excited that you're going to live here again! We're still on for coffee tomorrow morning, right?"

"Of course! I told Joe that tomorrow morning was the one time I wouldn't be available to watch Lily this week."

Brianna, Shelby, and Rachel had a long-standing tradition of Saturday morning coffee. It had started in middle school with Saturday morning hot cocoa, but when they declared themselves mature, they switched to coffee. Even when they lived in separate places, they still had the tradition, but it had to be over conference calls.

"I can't wait to have coffee in person every week!" Even sick, Shelby never lacked for enthusiasm.

"I was just thinking about how I can't wait to dig in and help with the treatment center. How is the planning going for the fundraiser?"

"It's going great! We've got lots of money and items for the silent auction donated already, and Faith has been lining up future staff members left and right."

"Whew! I can't wait to get up there and hit the streets to get some donations myself. I just need to find people the fundraising committee hasn't talked to yet. I want to finally be able to contribute."

"Brianna, you've been contributing already. I've told you how much the fundraising committee has liked the ideas you've emailed. They're all looking forward to you being at the next meeting."

"Good. Me too."

"Speaking of the center, Faith is calling now. Call me when you get here!"

Talking to Shelby had the desired effect. Helping with the fundraiser would make her feel like she was making a contribution to society while she searched for a job.

It always got her excited when people created solutions to problems. She knew that just like a similar treatment center had been instrumental in healing Faith from chronic pain and opiate addiction and given Rachel her mother back, this one would change families and communities as it helped the people who were trapped in the same cycle. She wished that it was already up and running and that there was a job that she could do there temporarily while she figured out her future, because it was exactly the kind of place where she could thrive.

Through her work and volunteer experience, she had worked with a few different populations who were in need of good, solid help and who were failed by existing systems. She had tired long ago of watching people fall through the cracks.

When she had started graduate school, she had big dreams that she would come up with an idea for a nonprofit that could truly be a help in people's lives, one that would support those who were trying to stand on their own feet rather than giving them a handout and a pat on the head that didn't actually change their situation. She had hoped that she could create something that would make a permanent difference in lives and families, the kind of difference that could last through generations.

"Okay, Lord, I know You are the ultimate difference maker, and I want to be a part of impacting families like that too. I know that technically it isn't possible to help the orphans, widows, veterans, victims of various types of atrocities, lost, and forgotten all at once, but I really want to help them all. Please give me one group or one way to help with multiple groups. Please give me some direction."

As she hit the two-lane road that would take her from the freeway north and west to the tiny town of Hideaway, she gazed at the huge pine trees lining the road and welcoming her back. When the urge to feel sorry for herself for being so directionless returned after a few minutes, she again fought it and forced herself to think about the things that she was going to be doing over the next week. She tried to call Rachel, then her mother and sister, and finally her sister-in-law-to-be, and no one answered.

So much for them distracting me.

Realizing she could do something for the treatment center while she drove, she called her brother-in-law, Quinn.

"Hey, kiddo! Are you in town already?"

"Not quite. I'm about an hour away and I can't wait to get home."

"Well, I can't wait to see you." Quinn had long ago gone from brother-in-law to brother.

"Me too, but I wanted to talk to you about something and didn't want to miss the chance."

"Sure. What's up?"

"Well, I'm helping with the fundraiser for the treatment center, and I wondered if anyone had hit you up for donations to the silent auction yet."

He chuckled. "Only Clay and Emily."

Darn it. They were both on the board of the center, so it shouldn't have come as a surprise. "I suppose I should have expected our almost-sister-in-law to start with the family, and I'm sure Clay has talked to everyone in town already."

"Yup, they both got me a while ago, and I gave them each a donation. Don't worry, I'll give you one, too, so you don't feel left out."

She smiled into the phone, then realized what he had just said. "Wait, did you give them a cash donation or a silent auction item donation?"

"Cold, hard cash. Why? Do I hear your wheels turning?"

"As a matter of fact, you do! I was thinking you might want to donate something from your site for the auction."

Quinn had started a side business selling local handmade goods online several years ago, and the business had grown quickly enough that he had been able to quit his job at his father's car dealership and focus on it full-time. People loved local products and would surely bid a good amount for some of the items his site carried.

"Hey, why didn't I think of that? That's a great idea."

The idea took flight in her mind even as they talked about it. "Is it a great enough idea that you would introduce me to some of your artists and let me talk to them about the center?"

For the first time in weeks, Brianna felt a sense of direction. Even a temporary sense of direction for a short-term project was enough for the moment.

"Absolutely. I'll swing by tomorrow and we'll talk about it."

"Awesome! You're the greatest brother-in-law in the world. I love you!"

Quinn hesitated and sounded choked up when he said, "I love you, too, kiddo."

It filled her heart to hear that he missed her as much as she missed him. Even though Quinn and Claire lived in Hideaway, and Brianna never let more than three weeks go by between trips home, she hadn't seen them since Rachel and Derek's wedding in February. They had always kept to themselves, but had recently gotten even busier with work and other commitments and had missed several family get-togethers.

"Hey, tell Claire to call me too." Her sister was hit-and-miss lately about returning Brianna's calls, but maybe Quinn had some pull that others didn't.

"Will do. See you tomorrow."

As Brianna ended the call, she made a mental note to set some time aside to catch up with her sister soon. Claire was busy with end-of-year activities at the preschool she directed, though, so their get-together might have to wait.

As Brianna was lost in thought, the phone rang again.

"Hi, Rachel!"

"Hi. Sorry, I was talking to Derek when you called. Are you on your way?"

"I'm getting closer. Just another half hour now."

"Yes! I can't wait! It's going to be so great having Saturday morning coffee together tomorrow. It's going to be different now that you're going to be here to stay!"

"It is! And guess what?" Brianna grinned as she took a swig of water.

"You're bringing Corey."

Brianna laughed so hard she choked on her water. She spoke through her coughs. "No, not quite, but thanks for making me spit my water out. Actually, I just talked to Quinn, and he's going to introduce me to some of his artists so I can ask for donations for the silent auction."

"Oh my gosh, that's a great idea! My parents will love it!" Rachel's voice lowered when she paused and changed the subject. "Hey, I wanted to talk to you before you got here to see how you were doing with the news about Garrett coming back."

Brianna sighed. "Rachel, you know The Rule. I kept it and didn't mention Derek when you were broken up, and you need to keep it now. The other day was an exception, because it was an emergency and you had to give me news." She wished she could go back to the time when he wasn't brought back to the front of her mind—not that he stayed far from the back of it before that.

"Brianna, come on. The Rule isn't helping you any more than it helped me. And I'm just asking if you're going to be okay, but you just gave me your answer."

"Next topic, please." She spoke in a light-hearted tone, but if the subject didn't change soon, she would be "coincidentally" hitting a dead zone with no cell signal and ending the call.

Rachel was kind as she went on. "Okay I won't push the conversation, but you need to know that five minutes ago when I was on the phone with Derek, Garrett showed up at his office."

Chapter 11

GARRETT SIGHED IN RELIEF when his old friend grinned and gestured for him to walk into his small office. He wasn't sure what kind of welcome he would get since he had cut off contact with him just like he had everyone else in Hideaway.

"Hey man, good to see you! I heard you were coming to town."

"I'm sorry I haven't been in touch."

"You know you don't have to explain or apologize to me. I know you had to get out of here." Derek waved him in the direction of the chair across from his desk as he stood in the doorway. "I was just about to get a cup of coffee. Can I get you one?"

"That would be great." He looked around the office as he waited for Derek to return. Derek had been the closest thing to a brother Garrett had ever had, and it felt good to be welcomed back.

Derek returned quickly with two steaming mugs. "I'm glad you stopped by. I was sorry to hear about your dad."

Garrett accepted the coffee, and Derek sat back down at his desk.

"Yeah. It's pretty weird to see him looking so old and weak in that hospital bed."

"I went through that with my dad last fall. Heart attack."

"I had no idea. Is he . . .?" Derek's father was a great man and had always been everything Garrett wished for and lacked from his own.

"He's doing great now. You won't be surprised that my mom whipped him into shape."

Garrett chuckled. "No, I'm not surprised. I'm glad he's doing well."

"I hope you can see him while you're here. You've always been part of the family."

"Well, I didn't act like it. When I left my dad and . . ." He cleared his throat. "Everything else in Hideaway, I left you behind too. I'm sorry. I just had to get far away from here."

Derek leaned on his desk. "Look, I don't know what happened between you and your dad, but I knew that if you needed to get away that badly, there was a reason. I prayed for you and trusted that God would bring you back at some point."

It was time to stop covering for Dad. He wanted Derek to know that he hadn't just left everything behind for no good reason.

Garrett leaned forward and ran his hand through his hair. "I found proof that my dad had been lying and manipulating me for years. When I confronted him, he acted like it was no big deal, then basically challenged me to a fight. I knew that if I didn't walk out that door, I would accept the challenge."

When he looked back at his old friend, he saw nothing but understanding in his eyes. "That was the final straw with God too. He had allowed my mom to get the blood infection and die and my dad to deceive me and . . ." He wasn't going to speak Brianna's name, so he left what happened with her from his list and cleared his throat again. Derek knew full well what had happened anyway. At least he knew most of it.

"When I left town that day, I swore I was done with both my earthly and heavenly fathers. On the day I finished school, I put everything that meant anything to me in my car and just started driving. When there was no road left and I found myself on a beach in California, I thought I was in the right place. The ocean was as calming as Lake Michigan always has been, and it was a great place for an angry young man with a college degree he had no intention of using and nowhere better to go."

Derek nodded. "I heard from Laci that you ended up out there."

"Yep." He took a swig of his coffee to swallow down the memories of the pain. "You know how much I hate big cities and all that goes with them, so I stayed as close to the beach as I could. Working in an overpriced restaurant at night helped me to stash away some money and surf every morning."

"I'm assuming you didn't find what you were looking for there since you didn't stay for long."

"No. I thought I could forget about everything here and start over. When that didn't work, I decided to get as far away as possible."

"I heard you went to Australia?"

Garrett appreciated the understanding in his friend's voice. "Yeah. It was great at first, but I still couldn't get away from my misery. Finally a man I had never seen before walked up to me and said that even though he didn't know me, he knew God, and God had told him to tell me He was waiting for me to come back to Him." He couldn't keep the grin from his face as he remembered his first meeting with Isaiah.

"Yeah?" Derek leaned forward. He had always loved a good God story.

"It turned out that man was a Ugandan missionary on furlough. God pulled me back to Himself on that beach in Queensland and took me to Africa to help build well pumps in small villages. I finally reached out to Laci from there and apologized for leaving her behind along with everything else."

Derek smirked. "How'd that go?"

He chuckled as he remembered the conversation with her. "She gave me an earful, but fortunately she inherited my mom's ability to forgive. And now I'm back here for six weeks and have a lot of making up to do."

"You don't have any making up to do with me." He suddenly laughed. "Actually, you did miss my wedding, so maybe you do have some making up to do."

"Sorry about that, man. I'm sure it was great."

"It was." Derek grinned as he took another gulp of coffee and stole a glance at the wedding picture on his desk. "Anyway, I always figured you needed to go your own way, but that you would come back some day. Look at how God used everything though. It sounds like you even ended up using that mechanical engineering degree you hated so much in Africa."

Garrett smiled as he pictured his adopted home. "I did, and building well pumps that would last for more than a few years was way more rewarding than designing car parts in Detroit ever would have been. We're giving people life there."

"And you're going back?"

Garrett looked down as he nodded. "I am. It's home now, and I still feel like I need to be away from here. There are too many memories. I'm just here to help Laci and then I'll be on my way."

"Well, we're just going to have to see you while you're here. Come on over for dinner some night. Rachel is a great cook, and I'm pretty good at the grill."

He grinned at his old friend. "I appreciate the invitation, and I would love to see you manage an open flame. Laci seems to want to be at the hospital as much as possible, and I think I need to be there with her. I'll let you know when things settle down a little bit there and I can make a commitment."

Derek smiled. "Okay, I'm holding you to it. Bring Laci, too, if she would like to join us."

Garrett drained his cup as he stood. "I'm sorry I can't stay, but I promised Laci we would go back to the hospital. I just didn't want to wait to see you."

Derek came around the desk and hugged him. “Thanks for stopping by, man. It’s good to have you back.”

As they slapped each other’s backs and parted ways, it felt as if everything was going to be okay. Eventually.

Chapter 12

As Brianna got close to her parents' house, she noticed several cars lining the street. That was a typical sight during the summer when beachgoers were coming to spend the day on Lake Michigan, but it was strange that they were there so early in the season. When she got closer to the house, she realized she recognized those cars. As she pulled into the driveway her eye caught the *Congratulations, Brianna* sign strung across the porch and her family and a few neighbors standing under it, cheering. The outpouring was so touching that uncharacteristic tears filled her eyes. She loved these people and was thrilled to be back living in their midst.

When she got out of her car, her three-year-old niece came running across the lawn toward her with a crown on her head, which was typical, and another one in her hand. The one in her hand had the letters MBA on it covered in glitter. Brianna wasn't big on crowns, but she was big on Lily, so she bent down and held her head very still while the little girl placed it on her.

She kissed her on the cheek as she picked her up and twirled her around. "Thank you for my crown, Lily! I love it!"

"We made it for you!" Lily put her little hands on Brianna's cheeks. "Now you don't have to go away anymore, right?"

Brianna smiled and gave her a kiss on her nose. "That's right! I'm home now and don't have to go away for school anymore."

As she walked with Lily in her arms toward the porch, the rest of the well-wishers came down to deliver hugs and congratulations. Mom and Dad were front and center, taking her into a group hug after Joe retrieved Lily from her arms. While Joe, Emily, and the others delivered theirs, she looked around to see if Claire was there and thought for a moment that this was another family get-together that she and Quinn were missing. When she saw her making her way toward her out of the corner of her eye, she ran to her. "Claire, you're here!"

Claire hugged her tightly. "Of course I am. Congratulations!" Brianna held her a second longer, letting her know how much she had missed her.

Quinn stood back waiting for his turn, and Brianna shook her finger at him. "You'll see me tomorrow, huh?"

Lord, forgive me for feeling sorry for myself. Having these people here reminds me what life is all about. I'll find my direction and my calling and I'm going to trust You with it. Just for today, I'm going to set it on the shelf and enjoy the people I love.

"Someone tell me there's cake!"

The next morning, Brianna bounded out of bed. It felt great to be home, and she couldn't wait to get together with Shelby and Rachel. Throwing on a pair of jeans, sweatshirt, and baseball cap, she headed out the door.

Even though she was never gone for more than a few weeks at a time, she always drove down to the lake to officially greet it and look at the waves for a minute when she came back. It was too early in the season for tourists, so she easily found a parking spot facing the beach. The waves lapping gently at the shore and the cool breeze gave her a sense of peace and made her feel like she was really home. When she had her fill for the moment, she turned around and headed down Main Street so she could stop for a treat on her way to Rachel's.

Since it was a special occasion, she stopped to pick up some donuts at the bakery. Once inside, she stood staring at the trays trying to decide what to get. Rachel was a creature of habit and always got the apple Danish, so that was a no-brainer. Shelby was on an anti-inflammatory diet, so the dark chocolate gluten-free, dairy-free muffin would work for her. *I don't even want to know what they made that out of.*

For herself, she was having a hard time choosing between the powdered sugar and nutty donuts, as always. Reminding herself that she would have easy access to the bakery now that she was home and could always come back later for the one she didn't choose, she mentally tossed a coin.

A voice from behind her spoke. "Try the bear claw. You'll never go back to anything else."

The familiarity of the voice barely registered as she turned, laughing. She lost her breath, followed by her smile, the moment she looked into the face attached to it.

The one person in all of Summit County that she didn't want to see stood inches from her, and he appeared as stunned and ticked about it as she was.

Chapter 13

GARRETT FROZE. HIS MOUTH went dry as he and Brianna stared at each other in shock. Turning his gaze from her quickly, he pretended to study the menu until he heard her stomp out the door.

So much for avoiding her during the six weeks I'm here.

Even though they both looked away quickly, it wasn't fast enough to prevent her smile from searing into his mind. The hunger in his stomach was replaced with a giant knot the moment he'd looked into her blue eyes. The knot was quickly replaced by the familiar anger when he thought of the way she had walked away from him so long ago.

He wanted to turn and stomp out of the bakery, too, but wouldn't give her the satisfaction of looking like he was following her. Seeing her up close like that brought back too many memories and too much hurt and anger. Having to go and sit at the bedside of the man who was instrumental in destroying the relationship they once had suddenly seemed like a waking nightmare. At this point, he didn't know who he blamed more—Dad, Brianna, or himself for being so stupid.

Garrett spent the next few days trying to be helpful to Laci and looking for ways to pass the long hours at the hospital. The updates from the nurses and discussions about next steps could only take up so much of the day, and Garrett was thankful that Laci gave him her old phone, which he promptly loaded up with e-books.

He had also taken time to have an early breakfast with Derek and gotten caught up with what was going on in his life then told him more about the projects he had been working on in Africa. Derek was happy to know that after the angry phase Garrett had gone through with God, his spiritual life was once again on track.

As he watched Laci at the hospital, he started suspecting that the burden she was carrying was not only about Dad. She seemed to be sneaking a lot of texts on her phone and didn't seem happy about most of them. It made him wonder how long she had been wearing the dark circles under her eyes and sad expression on her face that took over when she thought no one was looking.

Chapter 14

BRIANNA SPENT THE NEXT week trying to rid her mind of the sight of Garrett standing in front of her. She hated the way her insides had reacted in the millisecond before she realized it was him. His sly smile had set a swarm of butterflies loose in her stomach that she was unable to stop.

She didn't remember the last time she had felt like that. Actually, she did, but didn't want to admit that the last time was also with him.

"Brianna?" Claire was staring at her with a curious gaze. "Where did you just go?"

She realized she had gotten so caught up in the memory that she had frozen with her curling iron midair as they got ready for Joe and Emily's wedding at Evelyn Glover's house.

"Sorry, lost in thought."

"Do you need to trade places?" Claire was holding Lily on her lap while Brianna put curls into her hair.

"No, I'm good." She tried to sound casual. "My mind just wandered for a second."

Claire chuckled. "What's his name?"

Garrett's tan, smiling face and twinkling hazel eyes reappeared in her head.

So did the knot in her stomach.

So did her scowl.

"There's no guy, Claire."

Claire winked. "If you say so."

No. There's no guy. Please, Lord, take his face out of my brain. Despite her protests, he had become a permanent resident there over the days since their run-in at the bakery.

"Okay, Lily. Close your eyes while I spray your hair."

Lily covered her face with her hands while Brianna and Claire worked in tandem to glue every lock into place. Emily looked on approvingly as the same thing was being done to her hair. She dabbed her eyes as she watched her future daughter, and it was obvious that she was as excited about becoming Lily's mother as she was about marrying Joe. Claire and Brianna exchanged a knowing smile, and Claire gave Lily an extra squeeze and kiss. Their time as maternal stand-ins had come to an end.

They couldn't be happier for Joe and Lily, and now Emily. Emily had blended into the family flawlessly, and she teased Brianna regularly about the grilling she had given her when they first met. Brianna was a protective sister and aunt and needed to see for herself that Emily was a quality person before she gave her blessing. Seeing how she couldn't take her eyes off Lily confirmed Brianna's sense that Joe had found the right woman.

Derek and Rachel walked in just as the last of the hair spray dissipated into the air. Derek had duties as unofficial photographer and immediately began assessing the light in the elegant parlor, then he and Rachel rearranged the furniture to catch the sunlight streaming in.

The new mother and daughter looked so sweet in their coordinating dresses. The matching necklaces, a gift from Joe, were the perfect finishing touch. Even Brianna-the-non-crier dabbed her misty eyes as she watched the photo shoot.

The reception at Bellows Vineyards was in full swing, and Brianna sat alone at her table, watching the happy couples on the dance floor. Joe and Emily were so caught up in each other that they seemed blinded to the fact that they were surrounded by a room full of people. As she watched the newly-married Rachel and Derek and the newly-in-love Shelby and Clay, she suddenly felt very out of place.

As if he had read her mind, Dad approached her and put out his hand. “May I have this dance, young lady?”

She smiled at him and took his hand. “I thought you would never ask.”

“Have I told you lately how happy I am to have you back home for good?” Neither of her parents were overly affectionate during Brianna’s childhood, but her father had gotten downright sappy over the past few years, especially with Lily. It seemed that watching Joe lose his first wife had given him a deeper appreciation for his family.

“Me too, Dad. Things are a little different than when I left.”

He looked around. “Someday you’ll have this too. I’m not sure that God has created the right guy for you yet.”

She frowned. “Dad.”

“Hey, it’s my job to think that no man is good enough for my little girl. Claire somehow found one that I approved of, and someday you’ll find one too.”

“I hope so. We’ll see.”

“What about that guy . . . what was his name? That one you ditched at Christmas.”

“His name is Corey, Dad. How do you not know the name of someone I dated for all those months?”

He laughed. "I've learned not to get attached to anyone you date these days. They never seem to stay around for too long."

"Well, I didn't ditch Corey. I just knew it wasn't going to work out, and there was no reason to continue on if it didn't have a future."

"And why did that one not work out again?" He had a teasing glint in his eye.

She grew solemn as she looked at him. "Dad, how do you know if someone is the one?"

He squeezed her a little tighter. "Honey, I wish I had an answer for you about that, but I'm no expert. I was blessed enough to find your mother at a young age, and I just knew I was a better man when I was around her."

"What if I'm just not cut out for that?"

His blue eyes blazed with intensity. "Now you listen here. You are a treasure, and any guy would be lucky to have you. Can I give you a little bit of advice from an old, happily-married man?"

"You're not old, but yes."

"The next time you're dating someone, give him a chance. As happy as I am to have you to myself because I think no one is worthy of you, I'm also a little bit sad, because I don't see you give men a chance since—" He cleared his throat and looked down. "Well, I don't see you give men a chance."

Her heart lurched, but she reminded herself that she didn't allow herself to react to references to Garrett.

"I want to see you have that." Dad gestured toward the bride and groom with a tilt of his head. "Look at your brother over there. No one knows more than him how things can go south or that things don't always last forever, but if he hadn't taken the chance with that blissful woman in his arms, we wouldn't be here tonight. He would still be living half a life as a lonely widower, and you and Claire would still be doing everything possible to try to make up for Lily not having a mother."

Brianna was rendered speechless, both by the sight of her brother looking so happy again and her own fear that she would never again experience that kind of love.

Dad beamed as he looked at the newlyweds. "Today Joe got a wife, Lily got a mother, you got another sister, and I got another daughter. This is a good day for the Callahan family, and it's all because Joe took a chance." He looked around the room, his cobalt eyes searching. "I would point you in the direction of Claire and Quinn, but it seems they've snuck out early again. Same story, though, right?"

She nodded and put on a smile for him.

He tilted his head and captured her gaze. "Will you think about it? Will you give the next guy a chance?"

"I will, Dad." She kissed him on the cheek. "Speaking of love, your wife is standing over there, and she looks like she would like to be out here with you."

He looked over at her and smiled. Brianna crooked her finger at Mom then pointed at him and mouthed, "Trade places?"

Mom laughed and met them on the dance floor. Brianna stepped out of his embrace, curtseyed to her, and walked back to her table.

Picking up her phone, she headed outside. Her fingers hesitated but she opened her text app and tapped on Corey's name. "Are you free to talk?"

Chapter 15

GARRETT FORCED HIMSELF TO go back into Dad's hospital room after a brief walk down the hall. He had finally adjusted to the time zone but was still exhausted by the routine of sitting in a hospital room all day and into the evenings. The short walk helped, but he was feeling stir-crazy.

Laci was sitting at Dad's side telling him the story about the time the family went charter fishing on Lake Michigan and spent all day fishing in the rain. She'd been exhausting herself making small talk and telling stories while he stared ahead blankly.

Garrett sat quietly on the chair in the corner and listened. Laci had spent most of her life trying to appease Dad and gain his approval, and it seemed that she was making a last-ditch effort now that his life may be almost over. She'd refused to take any days away from the hospital no matter how much Garrett tried to convince her to take a break.

Garrett was sure he was partly to blame for Laci's tendency to try to play peacemaker in the family. She had always tried to smooth things over when he and Dad butted heads, which was often. After Mom died, Garrett confronted Dad regularly on his increasingly bad behavior, and their arguing was a frequent occurrence in the home. Laci took it upon herself to try to make everyone happy and make them get along, and had made herself Dad's doormat in the process.

What had her life become since Garrett stormed out of the house so long ago without looking back or considering the consequences to her? Guilt threatened to overwhelm him as he realized that she had been left to deal with the fallout from him leaving and that he had left her with no one to prop her up or challenge her belief that she was supposed to take care of Dad at all costs. The once-joyful girl had turned into a quiet, even docile, woman.

It was time to repair some burned-down bridges—at least the ones that had fallen on Laci. He needed to find a way to at least make a difference for her during his stay in town. The old Laci was still in there, and Garrett was determined to set her free once again.

When he looked back at Dad, the man was staring at him. The stroke had taken away his ability to have any facial expressions, so Garrett could only guess what was going on behind the blank look.

Conviction hit so strongly that it made him tremble. *I need to repair this bridge too.*

Chapter 16

BRIANNA WOKE WITH A start. *What did I do last night? It should be illegal to text while lonely*. She groaned into her pillow, as if hiding her face from herself would do any good.

She and Corey had talked late into the night, and she had agreed to let him visit next weekend. Now that she had slept on it, she hoped she hadn't made a huge mistake.

Corey is a good man and always treated you well. Who cares if he is a little bit of a pushover and doesn't fight back with you? Your tendency to leave good men in your wake is a town joke, and you're going to be alone for the rest of your life if you don't give someone a chance.

Pushing the thought out of her mind, she quickly showered, got dressed, and headed out the door. She was helping Joe with a surprise for Emily and needed to pick Lily up from her other grandparents' house. Joe was a clever one, convincing Emily that the date he suggested for their wedding was based on his work schedule and the best time for him to take time off for a honeymoon. Brianna hoped that Emily hadn't realized that her wedding day was the day before Mother's Day, and she was excited to help him with the surprise.

As she got out of the car, Lily came bounding out of the house with her Grandma Mary on her heels. Mary beamed at the little girl. "She's been waiting at the door and can't wait to go see her daddy and new mommy this morning."

Brianna scooped her up and twirled her around, nuzzling her neck and planting kisses on her cheek. "Thanks for having her ready."

Mary laughed. "I couldn't have slowed her down if I wanted to this morning. She's still all fired up over yesterday's excitement."

Brianna was amazed at the woman's ability to be happy for her granddaughter getting a new mommy. She had been as devastated as anyone when her daughter died, but was one of the biggest supporters of Joe marrying again. She and Emily had even spent quite a bit of time together developing their own relationship, and it was clear that no one was being replaced in Lily's life.

Armed with flowers, the Mommy crown and Mother's Day banner she and Lily had made, along with a handful of cards for Emily, she began the drive to Joe and Emily's new house. The plans for their surprise had gotten much simpler when Emily suggested that she and Joe spend their first night together in their new home. It would be much easier to sneak Lily and the gifts through the back door of the house than into a fancy hotel room.

"Lily, do you want to practice your line?"

"Happy Mommy Day!" She giggled and clapped her hands as she said it, and Brianna hoped she would do the same thing when she said it for real.

"Good job!"

She reminded Lily that they were playing the Quiet Game as they snuck in through the back door and met Joe.

"Good morning, Princess," Joe whispered as he took Lily from Brianna's arms. "Thanks again for doing this, sis. Breakfast is ready, and all I need is for you to put the banner up over the table. Emily is still drying her hair upstairs, so your timing is perfect."

Brianna quickly set the flowers and cards on the table, taped the banner up, kissed Joe and Lily on their cheeks, and slipped out the door. As she drove away, she prayed for the new family. "Lord, thank You for creating that little family in there. Thank You for giving Joe a second love of his life and for giving Lily a mommy to love her and guide her."

She thought of her friends and the changes in their love lives over the past several months as she continued with her thanks. "Thank You for giving Rachel a new start with the love of her life, too, and for giving Shelby the answer to years of prayers and dreams about Clay. You've sure been busy around here lately."

She was hesitant to ask for her own happiness. It was scary to want that, let alone ask for it. "Lord, should I even ask for that? You know how much I want someone to share my life with and how much I want to be someone's mommy. Seeing Joe's new family just brings that desire back up to the surface and I want it too."

When Garrett's face came to mind, as was becoming a habit, she pushed it away and tried to picture Corey's instead.

"Please help me to give Corey a chance. He really is a good guy, and I think I loved him when we were dating. Maybe I've been looking for something that doesn't exist."

Garrett's face came back, and she was swept up in a memory of one of the last times they had spread out a blanket on the beach to watch for shooting stars. They had studied the constellations together and were arguing over whether or not they were looking at Pegasus.

"Say what you want, Brianna. You know you're wrong." He nudged her with his elbow and grinned at her. "You know that I personally love your stubbornness, but someday it's going to get you into trouble."

"Ha! Look who is calling who stubborn, Mr. Hard Head!" She couldn't stop her own laughter. "You'd better admit that you're wrong if you think you're going to get any kisses from me tonight."

She acted as if she was going to scoot away, but he grabbed her and pulled her close. She pretended to push against him even as she giggled, but she was no match for his strength.

"You know you like it when I steal kisses from you." And he did steal a kiss . . . and then another . . . and another.

As usual, she eventually became the one doing the stealing. "You're totally wrong about Pegasus, but I'll admit you're right about stealing kisses from me. You'd better steal some more to make up for the time you're going to be away."

"Do you want to know what I like best about all those stars up there?" He gestured toward the sky without moving away or taking his eyes from hers.

"What?"

"No matter where we are, we can always look at the sky and know that we're under the same stars. Even when I leave in a few weeks, we'll have that." He stroked her cheek. "Every time you look up, know that I'm looking at the same thing and missing you. And when I come home to see you almost every weekend, we can look at them together again."

"And next year when I'm there too, we can watch them together in Ann Arbor. You're going to have to scope out some good star-gazing spots for us this year."

"I'll find some for us. I wish we could fast-forward to next year so we could be planning to go away together now. And I wish we could fast-forward past college so we could get married and make the world better together."

"I wish we could too. We need to pray that these next few years go by fast. Maybe we can even convince our parents to let us get married while we're in college if our grades are good enough. Why should we wait when we know we're going to be together forever?" She dug her fingers into his hair and kissed him like it was the last time.

Brianna tried again to push the images of his face close to hers and the feel of his lips on hers away. His were the only lips to touch hers, and the memory was still strong. As if that wasn't bad enough, the butterflies were back in her stomach.

Knock it off, stomach. Whose side are you on, anyway?

"Lord, please erase him from my memory. He has no place in my brain or in my life anymore. 'Forever' from that day turned out to be three weeks, and I wish I could take away all of the things we said to each other. Please help me forget the feelings I had for him. All they do is torture me, and they weren't even real. Puppy love is just that. Help me to find real, grown-up, mature love with Corey."

As she looked up, she caught sight of Garrett and Laci driving in the other direction. She tried to crouch down in her seat and hoped he didn't see her.

"Was that supposed to be some kind of joke, Lord? Maybe my sense of humor needs adjusting, but I didn't find that funny at all. That's just another reason to work things out with Corey. I can move away from here and not have to worry about running into Garrett anywhere."

Tears filled her eyes as she thought about moving away from the town and the people she so loved. She couldn't imagine leaving her friends and family again, especially after promising Lily she was home to stay.

Oh, I'm so confused.

Chapter 17

GARRETT PRAYED AS HE worked on his speech in his head. He had never had any intention of speaking to Dad again and had always assumed that the next time he saw him he would be in a casket, so he needed time to figure out what to say now that he was planning to do it. After spending time praying and talking with Derek about it, he'd gotten the encouragement and insights he needed to start.

Okay, Lord, I know that I need to go into this with the right expectations. I know I'm never going to hear an apology from him for everything he did, and I have to accept that. I forgave him a long time ago, knowing that he would never acknowledge any wrongdoing and knowing in my head that I didn't need that from him. Now, even if he wanted to, he couldn't say the words I used to think I needed to hear. Help me to say the words that You want me to say to him.

While Laci was telling Dad a story about one of their family vacations to the Upper Peninsula, Garrett summoned his courage.

When Laci finished her story, she looked at Garrett. "Are you okay?"

"Yeah, I just need a minute with Dad."

She looked surprised but relieved. "Okay, I think I could use a little walk anyway. I'll be back in a while." She patted his shoulder as she walked out.

A few minutes passed after she left the room before Garrett could look at Dad. When he did, those blank eyes were staring at him again. He needed to take advantage of both the privacy and the brief time Dad would be awake, and he found himself wishing it could be a two-way conversation.

"Dad . . ." He moved his chair closer, readying himself. "I know you think apologies and forgiveness are for cowards, but I want you to know that I'm sorry . . . and that I forgive you. It's okay that you don't apologize or forgive and I'm not looking for that from you. I just want you to hear it from me."

For the first time since he'd started speaking, he looked at Dad. The scowl he had grown up with wasn't there. The blank stare remained, but his eyes looked somehow more intense, as if he was listening.

On the off chance that he was, Garrett needed to say more. "I know I was a real pain as a son, and I wasn't always respectful. I should have handled things differently when I thought you were wrong, and I'm sorry."

He cleared his throat in an attempt to get rid of the lump that had lodged there.

"In my own way, I loved you. I wanted to please you just like Laci does, but I always figured it would never happen, so I stopped trying. When I found out about the trust and the scholarship . . ." It took everything in him to keep talking and to keep his temper from flaring again. "Well, let's just say it was the final straw. I'm sorry things went down as they did between us though."

He didn't know what else to say. There really was nothing else. He was apologizing to him as an act of obedience to God, not as an act of reconciliation. He meant every word he said, but he was not looking for any future relationship. Dad was probably going to die soon anyway, so regardless of what he was looking for, a future relationship this side of Heaven was an impossibility.

As if trying to prove to Dad that he meant what he said, he squeezed his hand briefly before leaving the room. Laci was returning when he walked into the hallway, and when she saw his face, she must have gotten the idea that not only had he spoken to Dad, but he was spent.

"Garrett, why don't you take my car and leave for a few hours?" She put her hand on his arm. "Go ahead, I'll be okay. You need to get out of here."

He gratefully took her keys and headed toward the exit. He needed to get far away from the place, even if only for the afternoon.

Chapter 18

BRIANNA AND LILY GIGGLED as they raced to Brianna's car. They had just stopped at Shelby's for a visit, and Lily got to have a story with her and a game of Hide and Seek with Clay.

"Okay, Lily, what's next on our special Auntie Brie and Lily day?"

"Ice cream!"

Brianna laughed at her enthusiasm and stamina. Before the visit to Shelby's, they had played beauty shop and had a much-shorter-than-usual nap, and Lily was showing no signs of slowing down.

"Okay, we'll get ice cream, but we're going to have some real food first." She parked in front of the Big Dipper and thought about what kind of coffee she would get once she got inside. She definitely needed something to help her keep up with her niece. It was fortunate that one of her favorite places for ice cream in town had food and served good coffee.

As they ate their hot dogs, Lily recited all the flavors of ice cream she wanted to order when she was done. Brianna's mind wandered to her upcoming visit from Corey, and she wondered if she could make living even farther away work.

She reminded herself of all of Corey's good qualities. For starters, he was sweet and dependable and came from a good family.

Sounds like a golden retriever. He comes from a good lineage and he won't leave you. He'll obey your commands and will never wet on the furniture.

What am I going to do?

She refocused her mind on the qualities she wanted in a husband and a father to her children. She wanted someone dependable, kind, stable, strong in his faith, loving . . . . Golden retriever or not, Corey did fit the bill. Maybe if she really committed to the relationship, he would make her heart thump too. In the string of relationships she had left behind, the common denominator was the lack of spark and heart thumping. *The other common denominator is you.*

"It's time to grow up."

Lily paused her ice cream soliloquy to look at her quizzically.

Brianna chuckled. "Someday you'll know what I mean, Lily. We all have to grow up sometime."

Lily looked serious and spoke matter-of-factly. "I'm going to be a princess when I grow up."

"You already are a princess! You're our princess, at least."

She looked at her plate. "Do princesses eat hot dogs?"

"Absolutely."

And they find a good prince to settle down with.

Chapter 19

GARRETT CALLED DEREK ON his way back to Hideaway and was relieved that Rachel was working late at the library so he could meet for an early dinner. Derek's suggestion that they meet at their old favorite place for hot dog eating contests as kids put a smile on Garrett's face and made his stomach growl. He hadn't been there yet since his return to town, and it was good to have something to look forward to.

He was a few minutes early when he pulled up to the Big Dipper, so he decided to save a table. When he walked in, his attention was caught by a young girl who was laughing at something her mother had just said. When the woman laughed along with her and he recognized the sound, he gasped. *Brianna?*

His mind swirled. *Could she have a child?* He was certain he would have heard if she had gotten married or had a child in the five years since he left.

Since asking about her would have indicated that he had interest in her and her life, he hadn't brought the subject up with any friends or with Laci. Consequently, he had no idea what her life was like. He tried to see if she was wearing a wedding ring, but her hand was hidden from the angle he could see.

The emotion he felt took him by surprise. As much as he couldn't stand the sight of her, the idea of her with someone else made his whole body tense up.

Get her out of your head. She's not who you thought she was.

When she got up from the booth to head back to the counter, he turned to leave before she could see him, thinking he would wait outside for Derek and suggest another place to eat.

At that same moment, Derek walked through the door. "Garrett!"

He was stuck. Out of the corner of his eye he saw Brianna spin around and Derek caught sight of her too.

"Brianna! Hey, want to join us?"

Garrett froze, wishing he could disappear—better yet, that she would. *Great. This is the last thing I need.*

He suddenly wished he had been straightforward with his friend about his still-present distaste for all things Brianna Callahan.

She looked as stunned and annoyed as he felt, and she didn't look in his direction as she answered Derek. "I've got Lily with me, but thanks anyway."

He wasn't looking in her direction, either, but it seemed worse to him that she was the one ignoring him. *I've got way more to be angry about than her. What's her problem?*

The sting of conviction washed over him even while the heat of his anger burned in his chest. He apologized to God for comparing who had more hurt than the other. Fortunately, the teenager behind the counter was ready for Brianna's ice cream order, and she turned from the conversation.

Garrett handed what cash he had in his pocket to Derek. "How about if I find a table while you order the hot dogs?" Walking away quickly, he was relieved to find a booth where he could sit with his back to Brianna. Seeing her anywhere was annoying enough, but seeing the tender way she had with the little girl stung his heart.

It took him back to the days after Mom died, shortly after his fifteenth birthday. When she lost her short fight with the blood infection, Garrett and Brianna were in an "off" cycle of the on-and-off relationship they had been in since they were eleven years old, and "going steady" meant they liked each other but didn't actually talk. After Mom's death, Brianna had stopped by his house every day and even learned how to make chocolate chip cookies to comfort him. She spent time with Laci, too, explaining to Garrett that Laci's friends were too young to know that she needed them.

As she sat next to him at the memorial service, Garrett asked God to let him marry her someday. Later that evening, he asked her to flip the relationship switch back on and to keep it on forever. They were inseparable from that day until three days before he left for college—the fateful day that Dad meddled and changed everything.

Derek's voice intruded on his trip back in time. "What was that?"

"What was what?"

"The fire shooting out of both of your heads."

Garrett rolled his eyes and shook his head.

"Oh, brother. Don't tell me you two are still mad after all these years."

"I would have to care to be mad." Garrett grabbed a hot dog off the tray and shoved it into his mouth, hoping the conversation was over.

Derek chuckled. "Yeah, whatever. We'll just pretend you're not talking to the guy who spent three and a half years without Rachel and who had a lot of tense encounters with her during that time and move on. How is your dad doing today?"

Garrett ignored what Derek was insinuating and skipped to the question about Dad. "Same. In the rare moments that he's awake, he just stares at us. He doesn't have enough use of his muscles to glare or scowl, so he doesn't even look like himself."

"Did you say what you needed to say to him?"

"Yeah, I think so." Derek had told him about the tough time he had with his own father before his heart attack, and it was helpful to talk to someone who had been there. "I never wanted to see him again when I left here last time, so I guess it's good that I don't have to have any regrets if he dies. I apologized to him and forgave him more for God than for him, but either way, it's the right thing to do." He took another bite of his food as if to punctuate the sentence, and he chewed slowly as he pictured Dad in the hospital bed. "How was it when your dad was in the hospital?"

Derek looked down. "It was awful. But it was completely different because my dad hadn't been acting like himself. It was easy to forgive him and tell him I loved him, because I was talking to my real dad, not the guy he had become over the past couple of years." He took a slow sip of his drink. "My dad took his heart attack as a wake-up call and got back to acting like himself after it. I've been praying that your dad would take this as a wake-up call too."

"Except we don't want my dad to go back to acting like himself. We want him to start acting like your dad." Garrett laughed ruefully and shook his head. "I gave up on that wish a long time ago."

"Sorry, man. I'm going to keep praying for him, just in case."

"Prayers never go to waste, so keep them up. I'm trying to pray for him too. I just keep saying, 'Thy will be done,' because I have absolutely no idea how God wants me to pray for him right now."

It was true. He had long ago given up on praying for Dad to change. In the face of his medical condition, Garrett didn't know which prayer was more compassionate—the one for life or the one for death.

Chapter 20

BRIANNA WAVED AS COREY pulled out of the driveway and headed out of town. They had spent most of the weekend at some of her favorite places around Summit County, talking about their past and potential future. She didn't want to spend a lot of time around the family because she didn't want them to get their hopes up if she couldn't make it work this time. There was no sense in adding to her reputation as the Runaway Girlfriend. Mom and Dad were gracious hosts but made themselves scarce when they were all in the home. They probably didn't want to intrude or get too attached.

The best part of the weekend was the low-key dinner at Rachel and Derek's house. It was a relief to have less pressure to be sole tour guide and host, and Corey and Derek seemed to hit it off okay. With both of them working for family businesses, they had plenty to talk about, and they had even manned the grill together while Rachel and Brianna prepared the rest of the meal.

An evening like that was exactly what Brianna wanted, and it felt good to be part of a couple again. She had hoped that Shelby and Clay would be there as well, but Shelby wasn't up to a night out. Brianna had hoped that if Corey spent time around her friends and in her world, it would help her feel more invested in the relationship. They made plans for him to visit again in a couple of weeks, and she promised to spend some time thinking and praying about moving to Toledo, even though she couldn't imagine ever leaving Hideaway again.

She was exhausted from playing tour guide all weekend. After taking a nap, she headed to the beach to pray and clear her head at sunset. As she walked toward her old favorite spot for watching the sun go down behind the lighthouse, she started her conversation with God.

Lord, please help me see what to do. I know I should be with someone like Corey, so it just seems logical that I should be with Corey himself. A bird in the hand is worth two in the bush, right? She sighed as she summoned up her strength. *I'm going to do what I promised my dad and give this relationship a chance, but I don't know exactly how to do that. Love seems so easy for Rachel and Shelby. Why is it so hard for me?*

Memories invaded her mind again, memories of a time when love was easy for her too. She shook Garrett's infectious laugh and smile from her mind and focused instead on the uneven sand beneath her feet.

Please give me some kind of guidance and something to hang onto. And take away memories of puppy love that only try to convince me that fairytales are real.

She was so engrossed in the conversation with God that she didn't notice that someone was in her special spot until she got there. When the man looked up, fury shot through her.

"You've got to be kidding me. What are you doing here, Garrett?"

He looked surprised and irritated, too, but didn't budge. "Did you buy this patch of public property since the last time I was here? I forgot to check the land surveyor's office before putting my towel down."

She put her hands on her hips as her heart pounded. "You know this is my favorite spot. Why did you have to come here?"

His smirk was infuriating. "Don't worry, Darlin', I didn't come here looking for you. And excuse me for not being able to guess where you'll be anymore." His gaze turned intense and eyes narrowed as he looked her in the eye. "Of course if memory serves, it turned out I didn't know you as well as I thought I did, didn't it?"

She wished for just a moment that she was one of those women who could throw a good slap and get away with it. Fortunately, she was very good at throwing fiery glares. "Yes, it turns out you didn't. You should have, but you didn't." If looks could kill, hers would have at least broken a bone or two.

He rolled his eyes as he stood and grabbed his towel and water bottle. "I was just about to leave anyway, so it's all yours." The sarcasm with which he coated every word grated on her nerves. "Have a lovely evening."

Not about to give him the last word, she turned on her heel and started back toward home, fuming with every step.

Okay, Brianna, there's your sign. The love and sparks that came so easy before left burns and carried a price tag you're not willing to pay again. The only price tag with Corey is moving away from everything you love.

Tears filled her eyes as the full weight of those words hit her.

Chapter 21

GARRETT'S LUNGS HEAVED AS he finally reached the top of the bluff. He had been running before going to the hospital every morning for the last week, hoping it would clear his mind. So far, it hadn't worked. It hadn't even cleared the memory of the argument with Brianna last week on the beach, let alone years of memories of her and of Dad and the burden he felt over Laci. He had hoped that the steep sandy hill would take so much out of him physically that his mind would follow.

Between watching Dad slowly fade in a hospital bed, trying to find out what was going on with Laci and prop her up, and running into the woman who turned his insides into flaming knots, his visit to Hideaway was even worse than he thought it would be.

He missed everything about Africa. He had purpose there, and was busy all day, every day. There was no sitting around in a hospital room or feeling helpless to make things better for a sister or a father, and there were certainly no women making his blood boil.

He pictured his return ticket in his mind. *Only three and a half weeks until you can get out of this place and go home. You can suck it up until then.*

As he caught his breath and guzzled his water, he looked out over Lake Michigan. This was once home to him, and he never planned or wanted to leave for more than a vacation or a mission trip. Now he was as much a visitor as the tourists from downstate who came to town every summer.

He sat on the sand and thought about the place he used to love living in. It was as beautiful as ever, with the large tree-covered hills surrounding the town like protective arms and Lake Michigan at the end of it, but for him it was full of pain and memories he would like to extract from his mind.

On the day that he made the agreement that changed the course of his life, he had sat in the very same spot, weighing his options and making plans. Dad had approached him that evening with a contract in his hand—an actual typed contract—spelling out exactly what Garrett had to do if he wanted to go to college as planned three days later. Since he was seventeen years old at the time, he needed Dad's permission for everything, not to mention money for tuition. He was for all intents and purposes trapped. The options in front of him were to agree to what Dad was demanding or break the promise he had made on Mom's deathbed that he would get a college degree.

Dad thought Garrett was wasting too much time with "girls and parties" during his summer break, which really meant he thought he was spending too much time with a *particular* girl and his friends. It didn't matter that Garrett was working full-time at Summit Mountain, mowing the lawn, and doing chores around the house. It didn't matter that Garrett didn't stay out late or drink or do anything that some of the other kids in town were getting in trouble for. It only mattered that he was spending the little bit of free time he had with the girl his father didn't like and that he was enjoying himself.

The contract that was supposedly in place to get Garrett "back on track" and serious about his future stipulated that in order for Dad to sign off on him going to school and paying for it,

Garrett had to take a full course load, pursue a degree that was useful in gaining a lucrative career, maintain a high grade point average—and be single. It was also stipulated that if his grades slipped, he didn't finish his degree, he started dating, or he told anyone about the agreement, it would void it and he would have to pay back every penny with interest immediately. He gave Garrett three hours to make his decision and stressed to him that there would be no going back on it.

Garrett had no problem with most of the contract and wasn't surprised. Ever since he had scored ahead of his grade level on a standardized test in middle school, Dad had been obsessed with his academic performance. His grades were the condition upon which everything he wanted to do rested. Sports, social activities, and even youth group all hinged on how many A's were on his last report card. School was easy for him, so even when he skipped from seventh to ninth grade, he was able to keep up and maintain the grades Dad expected and Mom delighted in.

It was the social effects that Garrett felt. Skipping eighth grade meant not only that he wasn't in classes with Derek, Brianna, and his other friends, it meant that he was thrown into a completely different school. He only knew a handful of students at the high school, and they were all older siblings of his friends. Dad didn't care about that, and seeing how proud Mom was of his school success motivated Garrett to make the best of a difficult situation. When she died, he decided that he would dedicate every A he ever got to her. It didn't matter that Dad took credit for all of them, bragging that it was his heavy thumb on his son that kept those good grades coming. They were a tribute to her, and Dad could never take that away.

When Dad approached him with the contract in hand, he had a gleam in his eye, and it was obvious that he knew he had an ace in the hole. If Garrett followed through on it, he could brag more about his son doing well at an academic powerhouse, and he could get him away from the girl he thought was too mouthy and opinionated. Garrett wasn't the only genius in the household.

He had taken the three hours Dad gave him to make plans. The academic part would be hard, but it was doable. Being away from Brianna was another story.

They were used to seeing each other every day, and he had already been dreading being apart during the week while he was at school; he couldn't imagine not being able to talk to her or see her at all. He decided on that hill to take the long view of things. If he said no to the contract, he would have to get a job locally, and there was no way he would be able to save up enough money to go to school the next year. If he said yes, he should be able to pull it off, and the school year would be the sacrifice that would enable him to have the future that he and Brianna had all planned out. He was certain that he could pull off the agreement not to tell if he dropped the right clues to her.

Knowing his character, she would know that he was up to something and needed her to believe in him when he broke up with her. She would know it wasn't real and would wait for him; he was sure of it.

Garrett was certain that if he could pull off the first year and demonstrate that he was serious about school, Dad would relent and see that he didn't need to be single. He even had his argument prepared for the end of the school year when he would lay out his case and ask Dad to remove that stipulation.

His backup plans were formed that day on the bluff too. During the school year, he would take as many classes as possible and look for jobs on campus that would get him the most money in case Dad wouldn't relent and he had to pay his own way.

The backup to the backup plan was less honest, but he was fully prepared to execute it if needed. Since he and Brianna had been planning to go to Michigan together, she would be going there the following year, and Dad wouldn't be able to stop them from sneaking around. By then they would both be eighteen anyway and could elope.

The plan was doable and brilliant. All it needed was Brianna's trust.

Garrett gulped down the last of his water as he thought about the hope he'd had as he formed his plans that day and then the devastation when it all failed. As he sat up there so long ago, he had been certain that, knowing him for so long and knowing him better than anyone else, she would recognize all the signals he sent and catch their meaning. She would trust him and play along.

All I needed was her trust . . . and she walked away.

During that school year, he had sent what he thought she would see were clear reminders of his love for her and clues about what he was doing. To distract himself and stay as busy as possible, he had thrown himself into his classes and gotten a job serving at a high-end restaurant.

The day he arrived home for summer break, he proudly walked into the living room where Dad sat reading the news. He reminded him of the agreement, of his perfect grades for the year and Dean's List achievement, and his progress toward his Mechanical Engineering degree. As Dad nodded, smiling, Garrett was sure he had him where he wanted him.

"Dad, if I could do all of this while being completely miserable and distracted by thinking about Brianna all day, every day, I can do it with her there. I've shown that I'm serious about school, and I'm going to do what I promised Mom I would do. I need Brianna back though."

Dad's brow lowered. "I'm proud of you for buckling down and getting good grades, and your mother would be proud too. She would want you to keep focusing on your grades." He took a swig of his beer as he turned back to the news, as if Garrett was no longer standing in front of him.

Garrett's voice was pleading. "Dad, come on. I've shown you that I am focused on my grades. I can be with Brianna and do well in classes."

When Dad put down the paper and smiled, Garrett's hope soared.

"I'll tell you what . . . you go back to campus for the summer and take classes. Keep showing me you're serious, and we can talk about it again in the fall. If she's half the girl you think she is, she'll still be here when you're done with school." The phrase "done with school" told him everything he needed to know about the likelihood of further conversation in the fall.

As tempting as it was to argue, he knew it would be pointless. He finally realized what the real purpose of the agreement was: to get him away from Brianna. Dad had never liked her and always told Garrett he should find someone more "suitable," whatever that meant. The strong will and directness that Garrett loved in her was exactly what Dad so disliked, and he was not known to change his mind.

Garrett decided to call Dad's bluff and within the hour had arranged for housing and registered for summer classes. Since he hadn't mentioned the job in Ann Arbor to anyone, he waited until he was on the way back to school to call his manager and ask to be put back on the schedule. It was apparent that he was going to need to be ready to support himself sooner rather than later, and he was glad he had already stashed a few thousand dollars away. He wished that it was enough to pay back what he already owed Dad so he could break the agreement then and there, but it wasn't close.

Throughout the summer Garrett worked like a dog, counting the days until Brianna would be arriving on campus and their life could start again. He had even found the perfect spot to take her stargazing. No longer would he have to settle for thinking about her under the stars every night; he would finally be able to enjoy them with her.

It still hit him like a fresh punch in the gut to remember finding out that she had enrolled elsewhere and wouldn't be joining him at Michigan after all. Over the months he hadn't heard from her, he had foolishly assumed that she was going along with the plan and not risking exposure. He couldn't have been more wrong.

No wonder he stayed away from women. They were nothing but heartache and trouble, and her kind was the worst. After the way she had been there for him when Mom died, he thought they could read each other's minds and would always be in sync. She let him think she loved him but then split when the going got tough and he needed her trust the most.

As awful as it had been living without her in those days, he was glad to be over her now. Her attitude on the beach last week was all he needed to be done with her calling the shots during his visit to Hideaway.

If she thought she was going to run him out of every place in town while he was here, she needed to think again. He was done trying to stay out of her way, and she was just going to have to deal with it.

Now that he had wrapped things up in his mind with Dad and with her, he needed to focus on Laci. He had three and a half weeks to make up for leaving her and to help her get on solid footing and back to the girl he used to know. Laci was the one stumbling block to him using that return ticket.

Chapter 22

BRIANNA AND QUINN EXCHANGED a high five as they walked out of the art center. He had introduced her to a few more local artists, and one of them had agreed to donate a beautiful pottery vase for the silent auction at the treatment center's fundraiser.

"I think maybe I'm getting better at sales. That was one out of three that donated this time!" As she laughed, Quinn shook his head.

"You're getting better at getting *donations* because you're *not* trying to sell anything. You're just telling them about a place that's going to make a huge difference in people's lives and asking them to be a part of it." Like the true gentleman he was, he opened her door and waited for her to get into his car. "Your belief in the center and understanding of what they do is what's making the difference. I can tell that all the artists we've talked to really like you, and I won't be surprised if you get some calls from people wanting to donate as the fundraiser gets closer."

"It's a good thing that I sprung for five hundred business cards, because I've been passing them out like candy." She sank into the car and grabbed her iced coffee. "Thank you again for taking me along on some of these visits, Quinn. I can tell the artists all trust you."

He smiled as he started the car. "It took a while to build relationships with some of them, but once they saw that I was offering a service to help them make a living off what they loved to do and not trying to take advantage of them, they came around." He paused and looked at her pointedly. "I don't sell them anything either. I just tell them about my site and tell them what the possibilities are with selling through an online store that's also got the personal touch of a small local business. Once they put something on it and see how easy it is, they trust the site and trust me."

"You've got a good thing going." Suddenly she felt the wheels turning in her head again. "Hey, maybe you could start a nonprofit arm of the business! You could get someone to teach people in need some type of craft or art style and sell it on the site. It would give them a chance to start a new life for themselves. I can run it!" She could feel herself getting revved up at the thought of creating such a thing.

"Slow down a little bit there, kiddo." When she started protesting, he put up his hand. "It's a great idea, but it doesn't sound like an arm of my business. It sounds like a business of its own and a lot of extra work, which I don't have time for. Let's get through the fundraiser, and I'll help you start that afterwards, okay?"

She sighed. "Okay. I just get excited because I want to do something. I need to create a job for myself so that I don't have to slink over to corporate America."

He chuckled. "You're too good for corporate America."

When he pulled into her driveway to drop her off, he stopped and looked at her. "Listen, I know you're antsy to start something, and I know you're going to make a success of anything you do. I told you when you used the site for that project in your Entrepreneurship class that you were good at this, and I meant it. I'm serious about helping you create something after the fundraiser, but you need to learn this type of business before you go off half-cocked."

He didn't react to her playful eye roll. "Tomorrow when we drive up to Northern Bay, bring a notepad or your computer or something. I'll tell you more about how I got the business off the ground, and you can start working on ideas for how a nonprofit might do something similar. You can start gathering ideas now and I'll carve out some time to help you after the fundraiser. I'll even introduce you to my tech guy and you can convince him to set up the infrastructure. Deal?"

He offered his right hand, which she took and gave a firm squeeze. "Deal."

As she got out of the car, she turned around. "Do you want to come in? You've hardly been over lately."

Frowning, he declined. "Can't. I have to go back to work for a few hours. I told you I didn't have a lot of time lately." He gave her a teasing wink as he started backing out of the driveway. "And now I have to go get ready to train a protégé."

"Future CEO!"

She skipped up the steps to the house. *I have my direction!*

After sending an announcement to the group chat with Shelby and Rachel, Brianna reminded herself that she should share the good news with Corey too. It seemed like a lot of work to remember to include him in her day-to-day life, but since she was officially trying to make the relationship work, she put in the effort.

He responded with a thumbs-up emoji and mentioned that it sounded like a business she could start anywhere. When he followed it with another that said how much he was looking forward to visiting her in a few days, she gasped.

I completely forgot he was coming! Okay, what do people who are giving relationships a chance do to pass the time?

She sat down on the couch and started a list of things they could do so there wouldn't be too much downtime on the visit. Last time there had been a lot of talking about the future and since she was not ready to commit to anything, she hoped to avoid that topic this time. Keeping busy would be a great help. She sent another message to the group text asking if Rachel and Shelby and their men would be available to fill up some of the time.

Once she hit *Send*, she turned the volume off on her phone and started working on her business plan for the nonprofit.

Chapter 23

GARRETT HUGGED LACI AFTER they walked out of the small conference room on Dad's floor. It was helpful to talk to the hospice rep, even if they hadn't come to a decision yet. He felt it was the right way to go and was sure it was what Dad would want, but Laci wasn't ready. Despite the evidence in front of them that he was getting worse, she still held out hope for a miracle. They walked back to Dad's room in silence, arm in arm, and took their usual chairs to watch Dad sleep.

Garrett was worried about how she would take it if—no, when—Dad died. It seemed like Laci was in a fight against time to gain his approval or love or something before he died. Garrett didn't understand it, but he tried to accept it and encourage her.

Dad wasn't the only burden on Laci's shoulders. It seemed like way too often Garrett had walked into a room and she appeared to be having difficult discussions over text. Her supposed boyfriend had still not shown up at the hospital to support the woman who thought he loved her. He also hadn't shown up at the house since Garrett had arrived, but she had disappeared a couple of times without explanation, so it was logical to assume she was going to see him.

It was going to take everything in him to not tell the guy off when he finally saw him, but he promised himself and God that he would hold back for Laci's sake. She was wearing out under the strain, and he was not going to be the one to push her over the edge.

As he looked at her, he knew he was going to need to change the date on his return flight. There was no way he could leave her in the state she was in or leave her vulnerable to the wolf she called a boyfriend.

Suddenly her phone buzzed and her face brightened. He hoped it wasn't something from Ronnie. He couldn't stand to see her get strung along.

She handed her phone to Garrett. "Look. It's from Zack, and he's doing better."

Zack Huntley had been one of Laci's best buddies since they were kids. He was away getting treatment for PTSD and help with a prosthetic leg after being injured in a war zone, but had kept in close contact with Laci. Garrett had always liked the kid and was happy to see good news from him. He wondered if Zack had any idea what was going on with Laci and Ronnie and if he had any influence over her. It was tempting to memorize his number and call him himself, but Laci would kill him if he tried to butt that far into her business.

He made a mental note to try to find out when Zack was coming back to town. It might influence his own flight plans if he knew there was someone else in town who would take a brotherly role with her. He wished Laci saw Zack as something other than a brother or buddy, but even though that wasn't the case, it was nice to see her smile for a change as she typed away on the screen.

Chapter 24

BRIANNA WAS GETTING A splitting headache. She was trying her best to stay in the conversation at Rachel and Derek's house, but it was taking everything in her to do so. The visit had been going well, judging by Corey's constant smiles, but she was once again exhausted. She had always thought she was pretty good at hospitality, but these visits were making her think she had deluded herself. While the strategy of making a bunch of plans so there wouldn't be time for a lot of talking was working, it was as exhausting going from activity to activity as it had been talking about the future she was trying so hard to make herself want.

They had enjoyed another relaxing meal with Rachel and Derek, but even with them taking some of the tour guide heat off of her, Brianna was ready to collapse. Finally, she asked Corey to take her home.

She was silent on the way other than reminding him where to turn, and she couldn't wait to crawl into bed. It didn't matter that it wasn't even nine o'clock.

"Is your head all that's bothering you tonight?"

"Yes, it's probably just from doing so much. Maybe allergies. Sorry. I'm not being a great hostess."

He pulled into her driveway and turned off the car, but didn't move. "Brianna, I didn't come here to see the sights of northern Michigan. I came here to spend time with you."

She didn't know what to say, other than to apologize again. "I'm sorry, Corey. I'm just trying to make it fun for us."

"Well, I have fun just being with you. I don't need canoes or bike rides or any of the things we've done. They've been great, but I was just hoping for some time for us to talk."

Ugh. More talking. "Maybe tomorrow if my headache is gone we can talk, okay?" *And maybe I can come up with some things to say.*

Why are relationships so stinking hard?

The next morning, Brianna was still exhausted when she woke up. When she finally got out of bed, Mom, Dad, and Corey were halfway through breakfast. Mom and Dad seemed to speed up their eating, and by the time Brianna had poured her coffee they were headed out the door. She looked at the clock and realized that church was starting in thirty minutes.

"Why didn't anyone wake me up to get ready for church?"

Corey brought his empty plate to the sink and leaned against the counter next to her. "I told them how miserable you were last night, and we decided to let you sleep."

"Thank you. I don't know what's come over me." She patted his arm to show her appreciation for his concern.

You're patting him like you would a golden retriever. She pushed the thought from her head, along with the wish that she could go back to bed.

"Since you're not feeling well, maybe I should take off now. Your new business venture is taking a lot out of you, and you should probably get some rest."

Brianna was struck by how sweet and kind he was. "Corey, have I told you that you really are a great guy?"

"Yes, you told me that when you broke up with me. You're not about to do it again, are you?" He was teasing, but looked nervous nonetheless.

I'm trying not to.

She laughed and hoped she didn't sound nervous. "No. I'm just sipping my coffee, trying to wake up, and telling you that you're a great guy."

He was out the door within the hour with a promise to return in two weeks for the fundraiser. Her shower helped her feel human again, and she sat in the back yard thinking about how to fill the time on his next visit. Helping with the fundraiser would take up a good portion of the weekend, and she found herself relieved that they would be busy and around people.

Pulling out her notepad, she started back on her task list for the nonprofit, which was growing. Her new business venture was not taking a lot out of her, as Corey assumed. In fact, it was energizing her like nothing else had in the recent past.

When Rachel appeared around the side of the house, Brianna looked at her watch and realized three hours had passed.

"Are you okay? Your mom said you still had a headache this morning and slept almost until church started." She sat on the chair that faced Brianna. "I brought you some tea that my mom swears is full of stuff to cure whatever ails you."

"Thanks. I feel a lot better now. My shower and sitting out here working on ideas cured me."

"Are you sure?"

Brianna wrinkled her brow. "What do you mean?"

Rachel looked as if she was trying to soft pedal a bit. "Are you sure you don't feel better because Corey left?"

Brianna's face fell. "Of course not! I'm trying so hard to make his visits here good ones, and I think I'm just doing too much."

"I know you're trying to give things a chance with him, but it seems like you're working awfully hard. You don't seem to be enjoying spending time with him, so what are you doing?"

Brianna felt tears threaten. "I don't know. I'm just trying to work it out. I'm reminding myself what a good guy he is and that he's got all the qualities I'm looking for."

"Well, most."

"Most?" She felt the headache creeping back up her neck.

Rachel paused for a moment as if choosing her words very carefully. "You always talk about seeing sparks fly with the couples you're around. Do you feel sparks with Corey?"

Brianna looked at the leaves in the trees rustling in the wind as she thought about her answer. "I'm hoping the sparks will grow over time. I want to be mature about this, and he's a good person to build a future with."

"You're right. He's a good guy and it's obvious he loves you. I just don't want to see you force something." Rachel held her breath for a moment before spitting out her next question. "Does all this trying so hard have anything to do with Garrett?"

"What? No!" Brianna almost flew out of her seat. "He hasn't been a part of my life for years. Nothing has changed just because he's back in town. Why would you even think that?"

"Umm, maybe because this is how you react when his name is mentioned." She cocked an eyebrow. "You're not over what happened with him."

The headache was fully back, and she pinched the bridge of her nose with her fingers. "Would you be? You never got over what happened with Derek, but you got lucky and found out that it was all a big misunderstanding. There is no misunderstanding between Garrett and me. We both know what happened. Case closed."

Rachel leaned in, and her face and tone were soft. "Brianna, do you remember the advice you gave me last fall? You said I needed to sit down with Derek and tell him everything that was on my mind and hear what his explanation was. You said we needed to talk things out and forgive and that until we did that, neither of us could move on, either with each other or with other people."

Irritation was starting to kick in. "Our situations are not the same, Rachel."

"No, they're not. But you two do need to put the past to rest somehow. From what Derek told me about what happened a couple of weeks ago at the Big Dipper, neither of you have done that. From what I heard, there were plenty of sparks there."

Brianna felt her chest tighten and couldn't help but roll her eyes. "Hate sparks aren't the kind I'm looking for."

"And they're not the only kind you've had with him. Just talk to him, Brianna. You owe it to yourself to get free from this."

"Ugh." She stood up from her chair. "Let's talk about something else. Are your parents ready for the fundraiser?"

As they walked inside the house, Rachel told her about all that Faith and Rick had been doing for the fundraiser and how close they were to being able to open the doors once the funds started rolling in to pay staff. Things were coming together. They had gotten the required inspections and permits, had the key staff identified, and Joe was heading up the last of the renovations to the old farm they had bought for the center. Soon they would even start the addition that would enable them to offer residential treatment.

After Rachel left, Brianna picked up her phone and saw that she had missed several calls and texts from Joe. The voicemails all said the same thing: "Call me as soon as you get this."

Her fingers shook as she tapped his name on her phone. It was obvious by his voice that something terrible had happened.

He answered almost immediately. "Brianna, where have you been?"

"What's going on?"
"I've got bad news."

Chapter 25

GARRETT SAT AT A coffee shop, enjoying the last bite of his sandwich. Over the few days since they'd finally had Dad moved into the hospice unit, Garrett and Laci had started taking at least one break outside the hospital each day. Taking turns ensured that someone was in the room most of the time and gave them each the break they needed. Since Garrett had convinced Laci to go to church with him before going to the hospital, he hadn't had to spend much time in Dad's room before leaving for dinner.

He was surprised when he saw that the nurse was calling. More curious than alarmed, he answered.

"Garrett, this is nurse Betty. Your father seems to be taking a turn, and you should probably get back here."

"Is my sister there? Is she okay?"

The nurse's voice was calm, probably from making calls like this regularly. "She's okay. She just asked me to call so that she didn't have to leave his side."

He stood and gathered his things. "Tell her I'm on my way. Thanks, Betty."

"Taking a turn" could mean a lot of things, but if she was calling him and asking him to come, it probably meant this was going to be the end for Dad. Tossing out his coffee as he walked out the door, he jogged down the block toward the hospital.

He didn't know how to feel. With each step, he fought a battle with tears. By the time he got to the hospital elevator, he was out of breath and the tears were close to winning.

A woman was kneeling on the floor of the elevator with her back to him, frantically gathering things that had scattered. It looked like she had just spilled the contents of her tote bag all over, so he got on his knees to help her.

She was sniffling as badly as he was as she scurried to retrieve her belongings. "It's okay, I don't need help."

He froze with the notepad and pens he had grabbed midair. "Brianna?"

When she snapped her head up and looked at him, her tears multiplied. Without thinking, he reached out and pulled her into his arms. His tears finally spilled over, too, and they kneeled there holding each other and crying for a moment.

"Brie, what happened? What are you doing here?"

She caught her breath as she leaned back on her knees. "Quinn was in an accident. He's in surgery, and they don't know if he's going to make it."

It was reflex to pull her back into his arms to comfort her the way he had so many times before. "I'm so sorry."

There were no other words to say. When Mom died, it made him angry when people used platitudes to try to make him feel better. From that time on, he had always tried to keep words to a minimum when others were going through hard times.

She was holding him as tightly as he held her. It seemed that they realized what they were doing at the same time, and they both pulled back out of the embrace.

He went back to picking up her belongings while she picked up a tissue and wiped her nose. As he handed her things to her, he tried to offer a sympathetic smile. Earlier in church when his old pastor talked about not letting the sun go down on anger, he asked

God to help him to lay his at His feet. The moment he had realized what the nurse was saying when she called him at the coffee shop, his perspective had shifted. Suddenly the anger he had stoked for so long toward both Dad and Brianna seemed pointless and destructive.

"I'm sorry. Quinn is a great guy, and I'll be praying for a miracle." If they were still in high school, or still friends, he would be taking her hands and praying with her for that miracle, right there on the elevator floor. As it was, all he could do was send up a quick silent one.

"Thank you. I appreciate it, and so will he if he wakes up." Tears came streaming out again with the word "if," and his heart ached for her.

Suddenly she looked up. "Wait, why are you crying too? Is it your dad?"

He nodded. "I think it's the end for him. I just got called back in here."

"Oh." She looked to the ground as if unsure of how to react. When she lifted her eyes back to his, she looked genuinely sad. She reached out and touched his arm. "I'm sorry, Garrett."

"Thanks."

"Are you okay?" Her eyes met and searched his, and it felt like the years and anger that had passed between them vanished for a moment.

His fresh wave of tears surprised him. "I'm okay. It's weird. We knew it was coming, and you know how things always were between us, but I'm still sad."

He couldn't believe he was actually having this conversation with the woman he shared only mutual fury with two hours ago. He also couldn't believe how nice it was to have a conversation like this with her, with no weapons drawn. She had not only been his girlfriend for all those years but his best friend as well. When she walked out of his life, she left a gaping hole that had never been filled.

After handing a tube of lip gloss that had rolled under his foot back to her, he stood and offered his hand. When she took it to balance herself as she stood, he was glad he was holding onto the railing. She still had the power to make him go weak.

The elevator came to a stop, and when the doors opened, her dad and Joe stood there waiting for her. They looked shocked to see Garrett standing next to her, but focused on her as she walked into their arms and they hugged her tightly.

As the doors closed, she looked back at him. Garrett couldn't quite read the look on her face, but it took his breath away.

His floor was two up from hers, so he didn't have much time to think about what had just happened. There was no one waiting for him, and he walked quickly to Dad's room, hoping he wasn't too late.

Chapter 26

BRIANNA TRIED TO KEEP herself together as she walked into the surgical waiting room. Claire sat silently, staring at the floor and looking shell-shocked, while Mom sat helplessly next to her. Emily kept Lily occupied with books on the seat across from them. When Brianna approached Claire, they hugged tightly and cried together. Quinn's parents, brother, and sister-in-law were there as well, and Dad told her what they knew about the car crash that had broken Quinn's entire left side into pieces and left him with a serious head injury.

According to the police officer at the scene, a truck driver had been texting and crossed the center line. If Quinn hadn't swerved, he would have been hit head-on and most certainly wouldn't have survived. Brianna breathed a quick prayer of thanks to God for sparing Quinn's life.

When the doctor walked into the waiting room with a nurse at his side to talk to Claire, the family stood with her.

"Mrs. Millard, your husband is out of surgery for now. He's got a long, hard recovery ahead of him, but there's reason to be optimistic."

Claire asked some questions and he gave more details about the surgery that had taken several hours while Dad stood with his arm around her to hold her steady. The doctor was compassionate and patient as he explained that they were going to keep him in a medically-induced coma for as long as needed in order for his body to heal and strengthen for the next surgery. They were in the process of moving him to the intensive care unit then.

The nurse who had walked into the room with him stepped forward after he left and told Claire that she would be able to see him once he was settled in a room. She explained how to get to the intensive care waiting area and suggested they all get something to eat or drink to pass some time and prepare for a long evening. Brianna looped her arm through Claire's while the family walked slowly toward the cafeteria.

As they stood in the elevator, Brianna thought about what had happened in there an hour ago. It had felt so natural and so good to fall into Garrett's arms and to accept his comfort as well as give him hers. It was as if the past several years had never happened. As if they had never hurt each other.

Seeing his tears reminded her of the boy she once loved and planned to spend the rest of her life with. She almost forgot that he was the same one who left her without warning or explanation and who didn't have enough respect for her to be direct about it.

Rachel's words about getting closure with him came back to her, as did the reminder of her own similar words to Rachel several months ago. *Okay, Lord, I know I need to have some sort of closure so I can go on with my life . . . so I can go on with Cor—Corey! I completely forgot to tell him what has been going on!*

She put her hand to her forehead. *I'm terrible at being a girlfriend.*

Chapter 27

GARRETT AND LACI SAT on either side of the hospital bed, holding Dad's hands. He was only taking a few breaths per minute, and the nurse said it wouldn't be much longer. The time was short, and Garrett again felt the nudge of conviction to say something to him.

He moved his chair closer, still holding his hand. "I love you, Dad. I'm sorry we didn't have the chance to make things right between us, but like I told you before, I forgive you and I hope you'll forgive me."

He took a deep breath and pressed on, hoping he could get the next words out. "Dad, there were two people who loved you more than anyone else, Mom and Jesus. They're together now, and I pray that you'll join them. Reach out and take His hand, Dad. Maybe in the next life you and I will get along and won't be so stubborn or willful."

In the wee hours of the morning, Garrett and Laci left the hospital after saying their last goodbye to Dad. The forty-minute ride back to Hideaway was a silent one, and Laci was as lost in her own thoughts as Garrett was. It was comforting being with her, but Garrett found himself remembering the hours Brianna was there at his side after Mom died.

It seemed as if she was there day and night back then. She had sat quietly with him while his house filled with well-wishers and had snuck him out of the house for fresh air when the crowd made him feel suffocated. During the long walks they had taken back then, she had been nothing but encouraging to him and often just walked silently at his side. After spending time with her, he felt like he could go on and be the man Mom always said he would be. Brianna was his rock and he couldn't imagine how he would have gotten through those days without her.

He had thought he had settled things with her in his mind when he sat up on the hill last week and declared that she wasn't going to determine his whereabouts while he was in Hideaway, but the moments in the elevator seemed to change everything. It shook him to the core to realize that his anger was no longer the comfort it once was and that he needed to get some kind of resolution with her.

Their story felt far from over. More than that, he admitted to himself that he wasn't sure anymore if he wanted it to be.

Chapter 28

BRIANNA WAS TRYING HER best to focus on the file in the computer in front of her. She was thankful that Quinn had shown her around his office above their garage and that Claire had been able to guess the password to his computer. They had only had three days together talking in-depth about the business, but she had a dozen pages of notes in front of her.

She prayed as she tried to piece together what she would need to do to help Claire keep Quinn's business going smoothly in his absence. Claire's focus needed to be on Quinn and being with him at the hospital, so she had given Brianna free rein to do whatever she thought best. Thankfully the tech guy, John, was as helpful as he could be and was keeping the site up and running properly.

When Quinn had passed the four-day mark and the swelling in his brain had not reached a level requiring more surgery, the family added that to the list of miracles they thanked God for granting him. There was no way of knowing how long he would be in the coma or what state his brain and body would be in when he woke up, but the good news was that the doctors were saying *when* he woke up, not *if*. Although they didn't know what lay ahead for him, at least his survival was no longer in question. Brianna was determined to make sure he had the same thriving business when he was able to get back to it that he had before the accident. Her own ideas about forming a nonprofit were just going to have to wait.

Her phone buzzed again. She had been ignoring calls and texts all day unless they were from Quinn's artists or her family. The only thing that would distract her from trying to figure out and sustain Quinn's business was getting news about his condition. Since she had ignored several calls and texts from Rachel, she answered, figuring it was important.

"Hi Rachel."

"How's Quinn? We've been praying."

"Well, God is listening, so keep it up. They can't make any guarantees about a full recovery, but everything seems to be progressing as well as can be expected."

Rachel exhaled. "Good. Is he still unconscious?"

Brianna tried not to picture him in the hospital bed with his breathing tube and his limbs in traction. "Yes, they're going to keep him in a medically-induced coma for at least another week. Claire hasn't left his side."

"I'll bet. When Derek's dad was in the hospital last fall after his heart attack, his mom didn't leave once. Derek and Clay begged her to let them stay instead, but she wouldn't hear of it." Rachel paused for a moment. "So, today was Garrett's dad's funeral, such as it was."

Brianna held her breath, not knowing what to say or feel.

"I know we're not supposed to talk about him, but I thought you would want to know that he seems to be doing okay. I'm only telling you this because when Derek's dad was in the hospital, it helped me to hear that he was okay, even though we weren't speaking at the time."

Brianna exhaled. It did help her to know that he was okay, even though she didn't like to admit it. "Thanks, Rachel." She wanted to know if he was planning to stay in town or go back to Australia or wherever he had been living, but wasn't sure which answer she wanted to hear. She was torn between wanting to know nothing and wanting to know everything.

"He asked about Quinn and about how you're doing." It both comforted and pained her that he was thinking about her, and she stared at the floor of Quinn's office. "He also said that he saw you at the hospital."

Brianna winced. She hadn't said anything to Rachel or Shelby about the elevator meeting, partly because Quinn's condition had taken up their conversations and partly because she didn't know the answers to the questions they were sure to have about it.

"I'm sorry I didn't say anything about it. I didn't know what to say."

Rachel's voice was full of kindness. "Don't apologize. It's up to you what you want to tell us, and we've hardly talked in the past few days, so everything has been about Quinn."

"It was so weird. We hugged and cried together like we didn't hate each other." She shook her head. "It was just surreal. I don't know what to think or say about it."

"Wow, you hugged and cried? No wonder he didn't look like he hated you. Well, I'm not going to push you to say anything more about it. Just remember I'm here, okay?"

"Thanks. I'll talk about it when I know what to say. You're the best friend a girl could ask for."

"So are you. I'm guessing you would like to change the subject, so how is it going with Quinn's business? Are you figuring things out?"

Brianna's eyes fell on the notepad covered in task lists. "I think so. I've been fielding calls from his artists all day and they're offering to do whatever they can. Thankfully, Emily has been doing some of his accounting for the last few months, so she has a handle on some of this too." She glanced at the clock. "She's coming over in a few hours to help me."

"Good. I'm sorry I'm no good at business or I would be there now. Let me know if I can do anything other than pray."

"Praying is the most important thing. I need God to heal Quinn and help me keep this business from going under."

Chapter 29

WHEN GARRETT WALKED INTO the living room, Laci was crying again. And texting on her phone again. He wished he could smash the thing to bits after all the times he'd walked in on similar scenes.

She had shed a lot of tears in the time he had been home, and it was often difficult to know if it was about Dad or if it was about Ronnie. The phone was a big clue that it was about Ronnie at the moment.

He sat next to her on the couch and put his arm around her. There were so many things he wanted to say and questions he wanted to ask, but it felt as if God was shushing him and telling him to sit quietly and listen. She leaned back and rested her head on his shoulder.

"Do you want to talk about it?" He hoped using their mother's standard line would help her open up.

"I'm just sad and I don't know what to do."

"About what?" *Careful. Don't push her.* He forced himself to sit quietly when she didn't answer.

She sat up and wiped her eyes, then looked nervously down at the phone in her hand. "How long are you going to stay here, Garrett?"

She had finally asked the question he dreaded—one of them, at least. Part of him wanted to use his return ticket with the original date, but that was only two weeks away. He missed Africa and his life there; he missed the simplicity of that world. The other part of him felt compelled to stay to try to help her get her life in order.

"I'll stay as long as I need to and as long as you want me to."

He hoped she would be comforted by his words, but they seemed to disturb her more. She wouldn't take her eyes off her phone, and she was clutching it so tightly that her fingers were turning white. Alarm bells started going off in his head. He wanted to see what was in that phone.

"We have a lot of decisions to make and a lot of things to do before I leave."

She nodded. There was a cloud over her that didn't make sense to him. She was anxious, and he couldn't put his finger on why. Something wasn't right.

Knowing that she was not in a state that would lead to open discussion, he changed the subject. "Have you heard from Zack?"

He was relieved when the gloom over her lessened and she smiled. "He's been checking in with me every day."

Garrett thought back to what Brianna had said when Mom died about Laci's friends not knowing she needed them. He was thankful that Zack knew she needed him and showed up even in the midst of dealing with problems of his own.

"He's a good kid." He put his hand up in apology. "Sorry, a good man."

Her eyes were brighter as she finally looked up at him. "He tried to get a pass so he could come to the funeral."

Hmm, a pass so he could travel from Missouri to Michigan for a day . . . and Ronnie didn't even show up from across town.

"Wow, really? He's a good friend." Just as he was about to ask more about Zack and try to bring out more comparisons to the other man in her life, they heard a car honk outside.

"Are you expecting someone?"

Laci stood up and walked toward the window. Her shoulders slumped when she looked outside. "It's Ronnie."

What a classy guy.

When she walked out and closed the door, she turned slightly and Garrett saw a look on her face that only deepened his concerns about the relationship.

The fears in his gut skyrocketed. He strained to hear what was obviously a tense conversation in the driveway, but all he could hear was Ronnie's chastising voice, not his words. Looking down, he noticed she'd left her phone and the screen was still open.

After arguing with himself for a few seconds, he reached over and grabbed the phone. It felt like an emergency with the way she had been acting.

He looked at the texts she and Ronnie had been exchanging and saw the likely reason for his sudden visit; she hadn't answered his last four texts from thirty minutes ago, and he had probably run out of patience. The reason for her anxiety and questions was also there on the screen. Ronnie was pressuring her to convince Garrett to give her the house and was pushing her to find out when Garrett was leaving so that he could move in with her.

Over my dead body.

His promise of marriage may have fooled Laci, but Garrett wasn't buying it. He hoped she hadn't said anything to Ronnie about the trusts Mom had set up. Greaseball didn't need more reason to sponge off her.

They'd had no idea about the existence of the funds themselves until the day Garrett found the paperwork in the basement along with the scholarship papers the day he left home. Laci had given Dad the benefit of the doubt and assumed he was going to tell them when they turned twenty-one and could access them, but after learning of the scholarship deception, Garrett gave no such benefit. He had quietly held onto the papers until his twenty-first birthday and made sure Laci knew about it when she turned twenty. Swearing her to secrecy, he also advised her not to tell anyone about the fund's existence to protect herself from scammers and predators.

Garrett shot up a quick prayer of thanks for the fact that Dad had never changed his will and that Garrett was still the executor. At least he could protect Laci from Ronnie's greasy paws that way.

Thankfully, she stepped on the squeaky board on the porch as she came back to the house. Garrett placed her phone back where she had left it, hoping his guilt didn't show on his face. She didn't look at him as she walked over and grabbed it, then walked back toward the door.

"I'm going out for a while."

Garrett willed himself to sound casual. "Okay, see ya later."

That snake. It was time to figure out how to thwart his plans and protect Laci. The irony was not lost on him that Dad could have come up with a brilliant plan—or that in the past, Brianna always knew how to help Laci.

Chapter 30

BRIANNA THANKED GOD FOR the healing power of a good shower and cup of coffee as she laid out her notes and Quinn's computer on her dining room table. Every muscle she had still hurt after climbing the mile and a half to the top of Sleeping Bear Dunes a couple of days ago, including several she forgot that she had.

She had felt guilty leaving both Claire's side and Quinn's computer, but Claire insisted she take some time off from both to spend time with her friends. Since it was Shelby's first trip back there since her health issues started, she had begged Brianna to go. Shelby had only been able to go a short way up while the rest continued the climb, but it was still a milestone day for her and Brianna was glad to be part of it.

The only downside to the day had been seeing Garrett and Laci off in the distance as they also made the climb. The dune was large enough that they were some distance away, but it was still a bit disconcerting that they happened to choose the same day that she and her friends were there. She had begged God to keep their focus in the other direction and make them invisible to the others with her.

Even though she and Garrett had seemed to come to some sort of truce in the elevator at the hospital last week and it would be nice to see Laci, she couldn't imagine standing there socializing with them. She knew that wouldn't be the last close call and that the time was coming to have the conversation Rachel kept encouraging her to have with him, but she had other things she needed to focus on at the moment.

She was as prepared as she could be for the meeting with Emily in an hour to discuss Quinn's business. The two had spent hours poring over the operational details of the business and were making good headway. After re-reading her list of questions and notes again, she bowed her head and asked God to give them both wisdom and direction.

Just as she started praying for her own personal needs, her prayer was interrupted by a knock at the door. When she opened it and saw Garrett standing there, she lost her breath.

"Garrett!" She looked around, confused. "Hi."

He held out a single rose, obviously broken off her mother's prized bush. "I know you don't like flowers, but this sort of reminded me of you. I couldn't resist."

She looked at him curiously. "Why would this remind you of me?"

He smirked as he twirled and examined it. "Well, it's beautiful . . . delicate . . . thorny . . . draws blood easily . . ."

She couldn't stop the laugh that escaped, and she tried to focus on the rose as she took it from his hand. It was much safer to stare at the flower than his teasing grin that made her knees shake. "Umm, thanks?"

He shrugged. "It seemed like a good idea at the time."

As she carefully took it from him, avoiding both the thorns and his eyes, he looked down and jammed his hands into his pockets. "Anyway, I was wondering if you had a minute."

Deep breath. "Sure. Come on in."

He looked over at the dining room table covered in notes as she led him to the living room. "Am I interrupting something?"

"I'm trying to keep Quinn's business going."

"I heard about that. You got an MBA?"

"Yup. Finally made it to U of M." She felt her face flush and wished she could take back any reference to their past.

He bowed his head. "Sorry for the part I had in that getting put off."

"It's all ancient history." Even though that wasn't quite true, she didn't know what else to say.

"How is Quinn?" He rubbed his hands on his jeans as he looked around the room. Seeing his nervousness somehow soothed her own.

"Still in a coma. It's too early to try to bring him out because of the head injury and pain. Claire has been fighting tooth and nail with the doctors to give him the least amount of pain meds possible, so for right now, it's good that he's unconscious."

"He's going to be okay, though, right?"

Brianna was touched by his concern, even while she was trying to make sense of the fact that he was sitting in her living room. She felt like she was in an episode of *The Twilight Zone*. "We're hoping so and praying to that end. The doctors seem cautiously optimistic."

She raised her eyes to his. "Did you come here for something?"

He laughed nervously and looked at the floor. "I'm not completely sure. I was driving by and just felt like I should come talk to you, maybe to clear the air. I saw you all at Sleeping Bear the other day when I was there with Laci, and it was awkward pretending not to."

She felt her cheeks flush upon hearing that he had seen them too. "I guess that's going to happen if you're staying around. *Are* you staying around?"

The knot in her stomach tensed as she waited for his answer. Part of her wanted him to disappear so she didn't have to feel what she did around him, and part of her felt as if a piece of herself was finally back where it belonged.

"I'm not sure. Laci and I have some things to settle with my dad's estate, so I probably have to put off my return trip to Africa."

"Africa?"

He nodded. "I've been working with a mission group there for the past few years building wells in Uganda."

"Oh!" *Wow. Did not expect that.* "Last I heard, you were surfing the globe. How did you get to Africa?" Picturing him serving on the mission field the way they had talked about doing together brought on an unexplainable sadness.

His face broke into a smile. "I was living in Queensland, and God used a man I'd never seen before to tell me to get back to Him. I followed the man home, because I figured what better place to surrender back to God than a grass hut in Africa."

She chuckled with him, but was struck by the way he beamed when he spoke of it.

"You look surprised. We always said we were going to do mission work."

Her breath caught at his use of the word "we," but she tried to act casual. "I know. We just always talked about doing short-term trips, not living in remote parts of the world."

"Well, I was in a place where I needed to be as far away from—" He stopped himself short and took a swig of the water bottle in his hand. "I just needed to be far away."

"And what about now?" She kicked herself, both for asking and for wanting the answer.

"I still want to be far away." He looked down again and seemed to be studying his bottle. "I need to take care of some things here first. Laci is . . . I think she needs me."

"Is there anything I can do?" She kicked herself again. It was a reflex to offer to help someone in need, and she had always had a soft spot for Laci. "Is she okay?"

He held his breath for a moment and looked back at her. "Brianna, I know we're not friends, and I'm not doing a great job of making things better between us, but I think I need your help."

Tears started to form in his eyes and Brianna leaned forward. "What's going on?"

"I think she may be in an abusive relationship. At the very least, she's being manipulated. Something's going on with her, and I don't know what it is. I've been trying to get her to spend as much time as possible with me, but it's not helping to get her out of it or to let me in." He looked at her with desperation in his eyes. "I can't leave until I know she's okay."

"That's why you're here?"

He rubbed his face with his hands. "I have no idea why I'm here. I'm feeling panicked about Laci and didn't know where to go. I was driving around and found myself here. I'm afraid she's going to do something stupid—or already has—and you always knew how to help her. I know we need to talk about some things to put the weapons down between us, but right now all I can think about is her."

"I'll help you with Laci if I can, but can I ask why you had weapons drawn with me? You're the one who broke up with me and left me without a look back." She cursed the tears that were trying to form in her eyes.

"And you didn't let me explain and told me I wasn't man enough for you." His eyes looked hurt, but she could see the anger still in there too.

"I believe my words were that you should have broken up with me face-to-face like a man instead of stringing me along," she corrected him, feeling the tension rise in her chest. "I never said you weren't enough for me. I just wanted you to be honest."

All the hurt from so long ago seemed to well up within her. Being left suddenly by the person she had planned to spend the rest of her life with and who she had depended on more than anyone else was some of the worst pain she had ever endured. His cryptic messages only confused her and made her feel like a fool.

He rested his chin on his clasped hands as he looked at the floor.

As much as she still wanted an apology from him, she tried to refocus on Laci. Her feelings could wait if a friend's safety might be on the line. "Sorry. You're right, we can talk about that later. Tell me about Laci."

He took a deep breath, then told her about what Laci had been acting like and about reading the texts from Ronnie. It sounded all too familiar to Brianna after working in the past with several women who were abused.

"I'm sorry to hear it, Garrett. It doesn't sound good. At the very least, it sounds like she's in the kind of relationship that can become abusive."

"I was hoping you would tell me I was being overprotective and that I was making a big deal about nothing."

"I wish I could."

His eyes grew wide. "How do I help her?"

She gave him some basic advice about how to encourage her and avoid pushing her closer toward Ronnie and wrote down some websites that could be helpful.

"I've been spending all of my time working on Quinn's stuff, but I could call her sometime. I'll pretend it's just a condolence call."

Gratitude filled his face. "You would do that for me?"

"No. I would do it for her. You're the guy who dumped me, so I don't do favors for you." She was glad he looked up so he could see that she was kidding—sort of.

He looked relieved and chuckled as he stood up. As he opened the front door, he turned back to her. "Brianna, I'm sorry."

Before she could respond, he was out the door.

She flopped onto the chair. *What just happened?*

Chapter 31

GARRETT NEEDED TO RUN. He needed a big hill to take, at that. His whole body was tense when he left Brianna's house and he needed some kind of release.

After stopping at Dad's to change clothes, he ran as fast and far as he could before exhausting himself. Once again he found himself atop the bluff overlooking Lake Michigan. He spent several long minutes looking at the lake, catching his breath, and thinking about the two women in his life.

It had been his hope that Brianna would tell him his suspicions were crazy. He had also hoped that he would find words to fix things with her and that they could be friends again. Neither of those things happened, and he wished once again that he was back in Africa, where he could tell himself that he didn't miss anyone and that he didn't owe anybody anything.

Sitting on that bluff, he realized just how much he owed to Laci. He had left her to deal with a domineering, controlling man while he went and struggled with his own demons as well as with God. If she was indeed in an abusive relationship, she had been set up for it by Dad's treatment of her and Garrett's absence. It was time to do anything in his power to make things right and help her.

It was also time to figure out what he wanted with Brianna, once and for all. Sitting in a room with her stirred up every feeling he had ever had for her, and then some. She was just as determined, strong, and beautiful as she had ever been. Even more so. Despite the fact that he was still angry and they still had business to settle, it took everything in him not to grab her and hold her.

The hurt he saw in her eyes when she said she had wanted him to be straight with her all those years ago was like a punch to the gut, and he had to avert his own eyes to get away from it. As he sat there on the bluff looking at the powerful waves below, he admitted to himself that the pride he still had when it came to her was doing no one any good.

He had never had the opportunity to tell her about the agreement with Dad, because by the time he decided it was worth the risk to tell her and let everything crash down if Dad found out, she wouldn't give him a second of time to talk. Eventually, he convinced himself that he didn't owe her an explanation and that it was her fault for not trusting him. He hung his head low as he realized how wrong he had been.

Before he could be straight with her now and tell her what he should have pushed to tell her years ago, he needed to figure out just how much of a man he truly was. He needed to know if he was man enough to help his sister out of a bad spot before he could do what he should have done with Brianna so long ago.

It took hours to feel ready to run back down the hill toward Dad's house. Garrett prayed the whole way that God would protect Laci and give him the wisdom to use the advice Brianna had given him.

The weight of the world—at least of Laci's future—sat on his shoulders as he rounded the corner. He was relieved to see her car in the driveway and asked God again to help her.

When he looked through the front window, he saw the answer to his prayers. Laci and Brianna sat talking in the living room, and it looked like Laci was crying. He turned around and walked slowly around the block to give them more time and to pray for their conversation.

During the walk, he also asked God to show him where He wanted him to live once things were settled. As much as he missed his life in Africa, Hideaway was starting to feel like home again.

So was Brianna.

Chapter 32

As Brianna, Clay, and Rachel helped Shelby clean up after the fundraising committee meeting, Brianna tried to move as fast as she could. They had been holding the meetings at Shelby's because her aunt Evelyn had a large dining room table that could accommodate a crowd and because Faith didn't want Shelby to expend unnecessary energy. She was hoping everyone would leave quickly so she would have time to talk to her friends about Garrett's surprise visit at her house yesterday. By some miracle, the goodbyes were short and everyone was gone within ten minutes of the closing prayer.

Brianna waited until they got settled on the porch with fresh glasses of lemonade to share her news. "So . . . I've been dying all day to tell you what happened yesterday." When Rachel and Shelby turned their attention to her, she made her announcement. "Garrett came by my house."

"What?" They both sat with mouths gaping.

"It was so surreal."

Shelby's tired eyes perked up. "What did he say?"

"Not much. It was a short visit. He's worried about Laci and thought I might be able to help."

Rachel furrowed her brow. "I was worried about her at the funeral too. She looked like something was going on aside from losing her dad."

Brianna wasn't surprised. "I went and talked to her to offer some encouragement. Keep her in your prayers."

"What else did Garrett say?" Shelby leaned forward in her seat. "Did you two make up?"

"Ha! Not quite. We did sort of agree to talk about what happened with us sometime, but that wasn't the time." She paused as tension rose in her chest. "He's mad at me, if you can believe it."

Rachel and Shelby exchanged a look.

"What was that look?"

Shelby spoke for both. "We're just not surprised, that's all. What did he say?"

"Something about us talking so we can put the weapons down with each other if we're going to be seeing each other around town." She felt the pressure building in her eyes, but fought to keep tears from forming. "I don't know how he thinks he gets to have weapons. He's the one who broke up with me."

Shelby reached out and squeezed her hand, but it was Rachel who spoke. "I think there's more to the story of him breaking up with you, and when he told me about seeing you in the hospital, he looked really sad."

Brianna felt the tears and anger rise again. "He doesn't get to be sad. He broke up with me and wouldn't even just say it." She set her glass down with a thud. "I bought his lines about trusting him and truth coming out and holding on for months. What was that all about? I'm the one who got toyed with, and I'm the one who gets the anger and the weapons."

Rachel wasn't deterred. "When Derek and I talked to him about his dad at the funeral, he made some comments that made me think there was stuff going on between them that was far deeper than just not getting along. It made me think of the messages he kept sending you when he left for school. I don't think he was toying with you. I think something was going on."

"Yeah, well, whatever." She stared at the empty sky. "What's done is done. I've moved on."

"Have you?"

"Rachel, I keep telling you that this is not like you and Derek."

"No, it's not. But you've been carrying this around since he left. You were able to enjoy life because he was gone and you could push it out of your mind, but you didn't move on."

Brianna let out a deep sigh. "Yes, I did. It's ancient history, and I'm making a future with Corey."

Shelby squeezed her hand again. "Are you sure? It seems like spending time with Corey is more like a job than a relationship." She paused and took a breath. "You know, we like to tease you about being the Runaway Girlfriend, but I think every time you run away from a guy, you're running away from Garrett. I think it's commendable that you're trying to make it with a nice guy, but it seems like you shouldn't have to try so hard."

Rachel took her other hand. "We don't blame you. You know that when Derek and I were broken up, I only went out with guys who didn't thrill me because I didn't want to get hurt again. I think you're doing the same thing."

She knew they were right. "Okay, I do that. But so what? Thrills aren't everything. I need someone I can rely on, someone who is going to stick around. Corey has everything I'm looking for."

Rachel was firm in her tone. "But you don't rely on him. You never rely on men you date. Don't you want someone who is strong enough that you don't always have to be?"

Brianna scowled. Her head was going to start pounding any minute.

Shelby interjected, "Brianna, if the tables were turned, you would be saying everything we're saying." She giggled as she added, "But more bluntly. Really, though, I don't want to see you settle. If anyone deserves the right person, it's you. You are the best friend either of us could ever want and we want to see you happy again."

"I am happy with Corey. He's a good man." She couldn't look at her friends. "He's honest and dependable and when he commits to something, he stays with it. I'm working at making it work with him, and I'm sure things will grow. Maybe we'll have sparks and maybe we won't. Sparks aren't everything."

"Says the girl who never wanted us to settle." Rachel leaned forward, forcing her to meet her gaze. "Brianna, what do you really want?"

Her eyes filled with tears. "I'm trying to be happy with what I have, not what I want. I want to be with Garr—Corey. I want to be with Corey."

Shelby had tears in her eyes too. "You're an amazing woman, and it breaks my heart seeing you try to force yourself to want what you have. No one is saying you should go and make up with Garrett and live happily ever after. It just seems weird that you're trying to push yourself to love someone. That's not how love works."

Chapter 33

GARRETT SUMMONED UP ALL of his courage to go talk to Brianna again. He had been praying all morning and reading over the letter Isaiah had given him when he left him at the airport in Entebbe. He had read it several times since finally opening it last night.

Isaiah reminded him that when he was planning the trip to Australia that put him in Garrett's path, God had told him he was going to come across one of His children who needed Isaiah's help to get back to the way God had laid out for him. Pointing out Garrett's boldness and courage, he told him to embrace those qualities and use them to be the man God created him to be. He also spoke of people who needed Garrett and said he thought there was someone who needed his protection and someone who needed his strength.

Garrett didn't know who needed his strength, but he was sure Laci needed his protection. She seemed less fragile since her visit from Brianna, and Garrett hoped that the visit was the reason. Since Laci hadn't mentioned their talk, Garrett had no way of knowing if they were going to see each other again or what was talked about.

His palms got sweaty again as he walked up the porch steps, and it took him back to the time when he walked up those steps every day. *You're not here for a date, man. You're here to help your sister.*

Brianna looked surprised to see him again when she opened the door. Last time he showed up, he was as surprised as she was when he found himself standing there. This time he thought he was prepared until he looked into her eyes.

"Hi. Come in." When he walked through the door, she gestured to the living room, where he took his old spot on the couch. "I assume you're here about Laci again."

He wiped his hands on his jeans. "I don't want to invade her privacy or anything, but I wanted to see if you think she's okay. She hasn't mentioned your visit to me."

"When we talked, she was more interested in talking about you than herself. She's worried about you too. Or rather, about you leaving and never coming back."

Garrett searched her expression, wondering if she was also worried about that. "I'm ready to put off my return trip for her if I need to. Do you think my fears were warranted?"

Brianna looked down and took a breath before answering. "I don't want to violate her confidence, but I would still be worried if she was my sister. I don't know if things have gotten violent, but he seems to have some kind of hold over her."

"I wish I could kidnap her and take her to Africa with me, far away from that greaseball."

"Leaving isn't always the answer, Garrett." The pain was back in her eyes and he felt his face flush.

"Did we just change the subject?"

"I didn't mean to, but I guess it applies."

The look in her eyes made him wish it was back in the old days, when he could pull her into his arms and soothe her. "I'm sorry, Brianna. The last thing I ever wanted to do was hurt you."

She stiffened in her chair. "Then why did you? Why did you slink away and string me along? If you'd wanted to date other girls at school, why didn't you just tell me?"

Huh? "Is that what you thought?"

She glared at him. "You know what I thought."

He had always missed the fire she got in her eyes when she was angry, but forgot the way he reacted when he was on the receiving end of it.

The pressure in his chest was rising, and he responded with more defensiveness in his voice than he intended. "That I didn't want to be with you but wasn't man enough to say it."

"Well? Why don't you just say it now, Garrett?" Her knuckles were turning white as she gripped the edge of her chair. "Get it over with so we can both go on with our lives."

"I tried to tell you what was going on. You were too stubborn to trust me." He was shaking inside and his own eyes blazed when they met hers. "I told you over and over. How could you think I would suddenly leave you without a good reason?"

She crossed her arms and stared him down. "Cryptic notes isn't telling, Garrett, and stringing me along was cruel. Why on earth didn't you just say it?"

His blood was reaching the boiling point. She hadn't lost her knack for getting him riled up. "You should have known that wasn't what I was doing! How did you just forget my character? You like to say that I left you, but you were the one who tossed me aside."

"What choice did I have, Garrett?" Her anger remained, but tears joined the fiery darts in her eyes.

All of a sudden, he saw the vulnerable girl he left behind in those eyes. His anger turned to sorrow. He sighed deeply and bowed his head. It was time to tell her. "Okay. You were right. I wasn't man enough."

When he looked back up, he saw that his words were having no effect on her. The girl who used to revel in being told she was right sat there staring, waiting for answers.

"You said I wasn't man enough to tell you that I wanted to break up, but that wasn't it. I wasn't man enough to stand up to my father."

She rolled her eyes. "What does he have to do with anything?"

"He has everything to do with *this*. I never wanted or planned to leave you."

She looked past his shoulder the way she used to when she was too hurt to look him in the eye.

He dared her with his eyes to look at him, waiting until she did before continuing. "Do you remember the last day we spent together? The day at the beach?"

She looked back down and her voice softened. "Yes, it was the first day we both had off in a while and we spent the day on the beach making plans for the fall. It was a good day, or so I thought."

"It was a great day . . . It was a great day until I got home and my dad shoved a contract in my face." His chest clenched tighter as he remembered the smug look on his face.

"A contract?" Her brows wrinkled. "What kind of contract?"

"The kind that had a list of things I had to promise to do if I wanted to go to school three days later. One of the things I had to promise if he was going to sign off on me going as a minor and to pay for it . . . was that I would be single." He held his breath as he waited for the eruption.

"*What?*" She stood from her chair and started pacing.

He stood too. "I'm sorry I didn't stand up to him. I didn't see how I had any choice."

The pain he saw in her eyes was unlike anything he had ever seen. The strong, determined woman in front of him looked broken. "Why didn't you just tell me?" Her fists were balled up at her sides as if she was trying with everything she had to maintain control.

He was a fool. Shame washed over him, and he sat back down and put his head in his hands. "Part of the agreement was that I couldn't tell anybody. If I did, I would have to pay back every penny immediately. He had me trapped and he knew it."

After a few moments of pacing, she started to calm down and sat on the other end of the couch. He could hear the hurt in her voice. "But why didn't you tell me?"

He couldn't look at her. "I thought I *was* telling you. I was trying to give you signals that something was up without actually violating the agreement. I begged God to show you what I was doing."

He shook his head. "I was so stupid."

She stared off in the distance for a long moment. When she broke her silence, he was shocked by her gentle tone. "Why didn't I know your dad was that cunning?"

"Because that was the first time he showed that particular side of himself."

When their eyes finally met, hers were full of tears. "I know it's ancient history, but . . . why didn't you make me listen? You never backed down from an argument before." Her tears spilled over and her voice became a whisper. "Why didn't you fight for me?"

As he started to reach out to her, they heard a car pull into the driveway.

Brianna looked at the clock and jumped up, wiping her eyes. "That's my sister-in-law, Emily. She's here to work on Quinn's stuff with me."

He was disappointed to have to stop the conversation that was years in the making, but relieved to be off the hook for answering her question. *Why didn't I? Why didn't I fight harder with dad and why didn't I fight harder to make her listen?*

So much for my supposed boldness and courage.

Chapter 34

BRIANNA FELT HER NERVES settle as they arrived to set up for the fundraiser, and Corey parked his car behind Derek's SUV. Having people around and activities to do made her feel less pressure than on the previous weekend visits.

Focusing on Corey after Garrett's visit the other day was darn near impossible. She tried to put it out of her mind, but she couldn't stop thinking about what he told her and about what might have been if she'd known.

For what seemed like the millionth time, she forced herself to focus on the task at hand. Most of the boxes Derek and Rachel had brought were already unloaded, and once they all brought in the rest, they started setting up the room under Faith's direction.

It was good to have something to do and to be busy. Brianna had felt tense since Corey's arrival last night, and it was taking all of her energy to avoid the conversations he seemed determined to have.

When they were driving back to the house to shower and change for the evening, he brought up her nonprofit idea. It was as if he had a cheat sheet in his pocket with categories of both people in need and resources for new nonprofits in Toledo. He was dropping even more hints than usual about her moving there to be near him, and she wondered if they were in the same relationship.

How is it that he thinks I'm moving to Ohio to start a nonprofit when I'm spending all my time trying to keep a family member's business in Michigan going?

"Corey, you do realize that my brother-in-law is in a coma and I'm working like crazy to keep his business afloat, right?"

"I know you're helping your sister, but it's not like it's your business or like you'll be doing it forever." He seemed confused by her question and annoyance. "I'm just looking toward the future."

It occurred to her that he didn't know how much she was working on it because she hadn't told him. They'd hardly talked since Quinn's accident and hadn't talked at all about the business.

She felt like a terrible girlfriend again. She also questioned why she wouldn't have told him more. *He grew up in a small family business, and it didn't occur to me to ask him to help. Lord, seriously, what is wrong with me?*

"I'm sorry, Corey. I guess I've been so busy trying to keep Quinn's business thriving for him that I haven't told you what was going on with it. I've been working with Emily to figure it all out."

He looked hurt. "Why didn't you ask me for help?"

That's a great question.

The memory of what her friends had said about her not relying on men came to mind. She couldn't deny it. From the time Garrett left her, she was determined not to depend on a man she was dating. In all that time, she had dated nice men and good men, but never anyone who she would have labeled as a strong man. She was so against depending on them and being let down that she wouldn't even ask someone she was dating to reach something on a shelf or open a jar.

"Brianna? Did you think I wouldn't help you?"

She scrambled for the answer he was still waiting for. "Of course not. I know how busy you are with your new responsibilities at your own business. I just didn't want to bother you."

"Well if you need help sometime, just ask."

"Okay. Thank you."

Just ask. She couldn't help but compare him to some of the other people in her life. Dad had offered even though he was making trips to the hospital in addition to working at his own job every day. Emily had helped even though she was taking care of Lily more so that Joe could go to the hospital and work on the treatment center.

Derek and Clay, who were busy with their own family business, had offered. Rachel, who was a librarian and knew nothing about business, had offered. Both of Rachel's parents, who knew about business but were swamped with the details of opening the center, offered. It seemed that every person in her circle had offered except the one who said he wanted to marry her.

It wasn't just that she hadn't reached out to him. He hadn't either.

She shoved the thought from her mind. *Marriage is about commitment and shared values. I don't need him to help me with things and I don't need sparks. I just need better expectations.*

Her headache was returning, and she reminded herself to take something and make a pot of coffee when they got to the house. It was going to be a long night.

Chapter 35

GARRETT WORKED ON HIS elevator pitch as he pulled into the parking spot at Summit Mountain. Derek had insisted he come to the fundraiser, both as an opportunity to talk to some potential donors about the pumps he had been working on in Africa and a distraction from dealing with everything at home. It was good to be on some of his old stomping grounds, and he was glad that Laci had agreed to come with him. She needed the distraction as much as he did.

She still hadn't mentioned her visit from Brianna a few days ago, so Garrett acted as if he didn't know anything about it. It seemed like she was acting a bit more like herself, and he hoped it was because Brianna had gotten through to her and not because she was hiding it better from him. It seemed like there were less arguments on her phone, too, and he hoped that was another positive sign.

He and Laci both brought donation checks for the treatment center from their trusts. The accounts were modest but made it possible for them to have emergency funds and have a small supplement to their incomes.

When they walked into the foyer, Garrett's eyes were immediately drawn across the way to Brianna. It had been years since he had seen her in a dress, and he was reminded that even though she was tough as nails, she was also as feminine as they came. His breath caught and heart raced as he stared at her. She turned his way, and their eyes locked for a long moment before she looked away.

Garrett couldn't help but smile when he saw that it took effort for her to resume her conversation with the guy she was talking to. The smile was replaced quickly with a stab of jealousy when he saw the man put his arm around her shoulders as they walked away. It was apparent that the man was her date, and Garrett didn't know how to react. He had never seen her on a date with someone else before; he had always been the date.

"You okay?" Laci looked at him with concern.

"What? Sure. I'm just taking it in. It's been a long time since I've been here."

"They've done a bit of redecorating since you worked here in high school."

As Laci was pointing out some of the changes, Derek and Rachel walked in. Rachel immediately went to find her parents while Derek greeted the gathering crowd and introduced Garrett to several people.

Throughout the evening Garrett kept a close eye on Laci, and she seemed to be relaxing and having a good time for the first time since he had returned to Hideaway. He was glad to see her talking with Brianna as well as with Zack's mother and uncle. The more people she talked to who weren't out to use or manipulate her, the better. He even saw her talking with a couple of different guys who appeared to be single and showing interest. His protective instinct came out, but they seemed to be minding their manners and she didn't seem too into them.

Between Laci and Brianna, Garrett had to push himself to focus on his own conversations at the event. In very different ways the two women kept his attention, especially the latter. It seemed as if his eyes automatically sought her out, and she was around every corner.

As promised, Derek connected him with some people who were very interested in hearing about the mission projects, including some who had a special affinity for Africa. Garrett was glad he had taken Derek's advice and printed up some business cards to hand out, and he hoped the brief conversations there would lead to some help with funding the wells.

When the speeches were about to start, Derek motioned Garrett and Laci over to sit in the two seats he had saved at his table—right across from Brianna and her date.

Garrett grimaced. *Oh, this isn't going to be awkward at all.*

Though he faced the front of the room, he could clearly see the two of them out of the corner of his eye. He tried to concentrate on the people at the podium telling their stories, but Brianna was once again in the way of him thinking about anything but her. It was clear that her date was not just a date, but someone she was in a relationship with. Realizing she could be planning the future that they had lost made his chest tighten. He needed air.

Chapter 36

BRIANNA STRUGGLED TO HEAR what Faith and the other speakers were saying. Their stories were riveting, but Brianna's attention was being drawn across the table. She tried not to sneak glances at Garrett, but it was taking all of her strength. She wasn't used to seeing him from across a table, having spent a good portion of her life by his side. Refocusing on the man who was by her side, she leaned over and gushed about what a great story it was that they were hearing.

Much to Brianna's relief, Garrett practically ran from the table after the speeches ended. Soon Clay left to join a conversation across the room. Derek and Corey went to refill everyone's drinks and after several minutes of small talk, Laci walked away, leaving just Brianna, Shelby, and Rachel at the table.

"So . . . that was interesting having Garrett here." Rachel could hardly contain her smirk.

"I didn't notice."

Shelby broke into giggles. "You should tell your face that."

Rachel started laughing too.

"Okay fine, I noticed. It doesn't matter. I'm with Corey."

"Are you sure about that?"

"I'm trying to be." She felt the pressure building in her head again and started looking for an aspirin in her purse.

Shelby leaned forward. "You and Garrett were sending so many sparks across the table that I was ready to grab a fire extinguisher!"

Corey and Derek returned to the table just in time to stop the conversation that was starting to make Brianna squirm.

Derek turned to Corey. "In case you haven't noticed this yet, when we come back to the table and these three go silent, it means they were talking about us." Derek winked at his wife, who saved the day.

"I was just telling them how much I love you, honey."

Brianna raised her hand as if in agreement as Rachel stood, put her arm around him, and planted a kiss on his smiling lips. As the crowd milled about, Faith motioned Shelby, Rachel, and Derek toward the silent auction area.

Realizing she was alone with Corey, Brianna tried to convince her face she was happy to be with him. "Are you enjoying yourself?"

"Yes, this has been really interesting and a lot of fun. I didn't realize how much of a struggle it was for some people."

As people started leaving, Brianna and Corey started clearing decorations from the tables. She noticed Garrett in a deep and animated conversation on the other side of the room. Ignoring him, she focused on the task at hand.

Clay had whisked Shelby out early so she wouldn't overdo it and Emily wasn't feeling well, so she and Joe had left early too. Since they were down a couple of helpers, Brianna tried to work at double speed so they wouldn't be there packing boxes at midnight.

Knowing the place well from working there in high school, she went to the supply closet to get a garbage bag. As she pulled one from the box, she heard the door squeak behind her.

She turned to see Garrett walk in and close it behind himself.

"Garrett!" She gasped. The click of the door locking brought back memories of sneaking into the cramped room for kisses on breaks. "What are you doing?"

"Something I should have done a long time ago."

She brushed past him to the door, but before she could unlock it, he turned and braced his arms against it, holding it closed and effectively trapping her between them. Her heart raced as she felt his breath on the back of her neck. She had to hold onto the handle to keep herself upright.

"We need to talk."

She felt lightheaded at his nearness. *I can't do this.*

"I can't." Her head was spinning, and it felt like her heart was going to jump out of her chest.

"All those years ago when I tried to talk to you, I let you shut me down and kick me out. This time I'm going to say what I need to say."

Her resolve was weakening and her voice was losing its strength. "Garrett, you have to let me go."

"I tried. It didn't work."

"Try harder." *Lord, help me to try harder too.*

"I've literally gone to the other side of the world trying to forget you. I can't stand to be in this town, Brianna. Everywhere I look, I see you. Every day when I pass by the Delbridges' house, I remember our first kiss when we were playing Truth or Dare. When I go by the high school, I see the tree we used to sit under at lunch, holding hands and talking about our days." The memories flooded her brain with every word he spoke. "Even at this nice event with all these people, I can't help but look out the window and see the chair lift we spent so many hours on talking about the future we were going to have."

"Garrett . . ." She squeezed her eyes shut to block the memories he was stirring up.

"I've gone to the ends of the earth to forget you. It's not working, so maybe God is trying to tell me something."

All the hurt from so long ago rose within her. "If I meant that much to you, why didn't you tell me what was going on? You didn't fight for me."

He lowered a hand to her shoulder and gently turned her to face him before returning his hand to the door behind her. His eyes seared into her. "I'm fighting for you now."

She pressed herself against the door and stared at him, willing herself to breathe. He was so close she was sure she could hear his heart beat.

"Brianna, I know you like to hear these words, so I'm gonna say them again. You're right. I didn't fight for you. I wasn't strong enough, and I wasn't man enough to stand up to my father. And you're right that I messed everything up by not telling you what was going on. You're right and I'm sorry."

As his eyes searched hers, she looked down to get away from them.

"Brie, I still love you, and I know you still love me. Don't deny what we have."

"It doesn't matter what we have—what we had. It's too late for us."

Too late. I'm with Corey. It's too late.

"It's not too late. I know what you look like when you're in love, and I saw the way you looked at that guy tonight. You might as well have been looking at the family dog."

She bowed her head down. *Is it that obvious?*

"Garrett, no one finds the love of their life in fifth grade." She wasn't sure who she was trying to convince, him or herself.

He raised her chin, forcing her to look back into his eyes. "And yet here we are." His gaze was intense as he leaned even closer.

She knew that if he kissed her at that moment, she wouldn't have the strength or will to resist. Part of her wanted nothing more than to have him take her in his arms and steal a kiss the way he used to, to make everything okay like he used to.

No. He left you.

His voice was gruff. "That guy is not for you, and you know it. You're not cut out for that."

"I'm different now, Garrett. You can't be upset that I'm like this." Tears filled her eyes. "You made me like this when you left me."

She kicked herself for her honesty. He could always reach in and bring out her most vulnerable parts. She had no defense against it.

He had tears in his eyes too and looked so deeply into hers that she was sure he could see into her soul. "I'm so sorr—"

When someone jiggled the door handle, they both jumped.

"Brianna?" Corey's voice was on the other side.

Garrett held her gaze as if nothing had interrupted them.

She could barely get out a whisper. "I have to go."

After a long moment he sighed, dropped his hands from the door, and took a step back, all without breaking eye contact.

"We're not done."

"I can't." She could barely hear her own words over the thumping in her chest.

She turned and opened the door just enough to squeeze out without letting Corey see that she wasn't alone. There was no need to give him reason to be concerned, and she was not in the mood to answer questions about Garrett. "I found a garbage bag. Let's go."

Chapter 37

As Garrett pulled into the driveway, Laci's phone buzzed. Her frown told him it was Ronnie. After the conversation in the storage room and Brianna's hasty exit, he was on edge.

He had made his own hasty exit from the building soon after, but not before seeing the way she looked at him as he and Laci passed her. It was definitely not the way she looked at the lap dog she called a boyfriend, but as she stood there next to the guy, it was clear she had made her decision. Maybe the girl who always looked for sparks really had changed.

I guess we really are done.

He was tired of watching the women in his life make bad decisions. If only the one sitting next to him would start making good ones, he could use the ticket for four days from now, which he still hadn't changed.

Laci sighed as she read the message and shoved her phone into her purse.

"Laci, haven't you had enough of that?"

"What are you talking about?"

"That." He pointed at the phone. "The guy never comes around in broad daylight, you're always sneaking off with him, and every time you get a text from him, you frown. How are you not sick of that?"

She averted her eyes. "We're just going through a rough time."

"How long has this 'rough time' lasted?"

"You wouldn't understand, Garrett." He could hear the annoyance creeping up in her voice, and hoped she fought back with Ronnie the way she did with him.

"I think I understand plenty. What kind of hold does he have on you?" He knew he was pushing too much, and he tried to remember the advice Brianna had given him.

Laci fired back with a power that he thought was gone from her. "You don't get to come back here and be all over-protective when you left me behind, Garrett. You just went on your way and left me here without a second thought, so don't try to act like the big brother here to save the day."

As she got out of the car and slammed the door, Garrett sighed and dropped his head into his hands. *I'm not going back to Africa any time soon, am I, Lord?*

Not wanting to aggravate the situation any more with Laci and not knowing what to do, he drove to the beach. The lake was better than any drug for calming his nerves. He sat there alongside a few other cars watching the moonlight reflecting off the gentle waves and tried to gather his wits about himself.

Part of him was relieved that Laci had snapped at him. At least she still had some of her old fire in her. He just hoped she used it when Ronnie got out of line.

The memory of Brianna being so close in the storage room kept forcing itself to the front of his mind. It took over and prevented him from thinking about anything else.

"Lord, help me forget her. She's made her choice and moved on, and I need to do the same. She's right that she's different now. The girl I used to know would never settle for what she's got with that guy."

He shook his head at the thought of her living a bland life with a milquetoast guy. It grieved his heart to think of it, not only because he was missing out on her, but because she was missing out on the life she deserved.

"Even though there's definitely something missing in that relationship, it's her life and her choice to make. Lord, please give her the life she's meant for. I thought she was meant for me and everything we planned together, but she's chosen something else. Please bless whatever life she decides to build with that guy. Please don't let him hurt or leave her the way I did."

Choking on both his words and his tears, he couldn't continue.

Chapter 38

BRIANNA TRIED TO PAY attention to the conversation going on around her as she ate lunch with Corey and her parents after church, but Pastor Ray's words about the timing of God's blessings wouldn't stop ringing in her ears. When he had talked about not letting impatience drive decisions in love and money, she wanted to slither down under the pew.

She glanced over at Corey. Between impatience and wanting to get rid of the Runaway Girlfriend title, she had tried to make something out of nothing and was wearing herself out in the process.

As she listened to the way Mom and Dad spoke to each other, she realized that she was fooling herself when she tried to convince herself that all she needed was someone who had the right character and values. She wanted—she needed—so much more than that.

Mom and Dad had watched Joe lose his first wife and raise a child alone, and now they were watching Claire sit at the bedside of her husband wondering when he would wake up and what state he would be in at that time. Through it all, they relied on each other and were best friends. They may not be terribly affectionate, but they seemed to have a different kind of spark, a solid and real one. They depended on each other and took turns being strong when rough times hit.

She felt horrible. When she'd told Corey he was a great guy, she had meant it. He was definitely too good to be in a relationship with someone who didn't need him and who was forcing herself to be with him.

After lunch, her parents headed straight to the hospital to keep Claire company, and Corey drove her home. Knowing it would be better to get it over with and let him go find a woman who he could have sparks with, she told him in the driveway that as much as she wanted it to, it wasn't working out between them.

When she told him, he had sighed and told her he was relieved. He had seen the signs she was trying so hard to hide and knew she would have a terrible time leaving her family and her hometown. The last thing she wanted was to make him think he wasn't enough, so she set aside her rule against letting men she was breaking up with down easy and let him think it was because she couldn't leave Hideaway.

His car was barely down the street when she called Rachel and Shelby.

Rachel was compassionate in her tone. "I'm sorry. I know you wanted to make it work."

Shelby, always the optimist, had excitement in her voice. "Now you can find someone who can give you sparks!"

Rachel chuckled. "Yes, real sparks! Watching you try to rub sticks together to make sparks with Corey, I was afraid you were going to give yourself carpal tunnel."

Brianna couldn't help but laugh too. "Okay, you guys were right. I was just being impatient and trying to move that part of my life along. I need to focus on Quinn's business right now, then my own. I'll find love later."

"Later? Are you sure about that?"

That evening, she was writing in her journal about her past relationships and attempts to prevent another broken heart. She had to admit to both herself and God that since Garrett left her she had been trying to control her relationships and had deliberately chosen men she could steer. And she could walk away from.

Nothing she tried helped to keep her mind from the one man she could never truly walk away from. The way she had always felt with him was the very definition of sparks. He was the only one she had ever relied on and who she could let down her guard with. Her friends were right when they said he was the only one who was strong enough for her to lean on.

"Lord, help me to let down my guard again. He was right last night. I still love him too. I do, and I never stopped. Please help us to get back what we had and make it even more."

As she was grinning and letting tears of hope drift down her cheeks, her phone trilled. Shelby had sent a picture to the group text of herself and Clay with huge smiles on their faces. The sunset was behind them, and her hand was front and center with a beautiful new engagement ring.

"Yes! I knew they were right together!"

That does it. I'm not settling.

Chapter 39

GARRETT FLATTENED THE LAST nail on the squeaky board on the front porch. Doing odd jobs around the house all day had helped him to pass the time and to clear his head. Having things to pound with hammers helped him to get out the frustration that he couldn't think away.

When Laci returned from work, she offered to help and ran up to change her clothes. Garrett prayed the whole time she was in the house for direction and words that wouldn't upset her.

Almost as soon as she got downstairs and started helping him sweep the porch so they could put stain on it, she asked him again what his plans were. She wasn't acting nervous like the last time she'd asked, and he wondered what had changed.

"I'm not sure, really. I still haven't changed my flight back to Uganda yet, because I haven't decided on a date. My plans depend a lot on you."

Her eyes widened. "They do?"

"Why does that surprise you?" He kept sweeping to keep his own nerves calm and hoped it helped hers too. "I told you I would stay as long as you need me and want me to."

She stopped and turned to him. "Do you mean that?"

He stopped as well. "Of course I do."

Her eyes welled up with tears. "I don't want to get in the way of you going back. You love it there."

After setting the broom down, he led her over to the porch swing, where they sat together. "You're not in the way of anything. I do love it there, but if you need me, I'm here. I told you I was coming here for you, and I meant it. I'm still here for you."

Her tears spilled over. "I think I need you to stay for a while."

"Then I'm staying for a while."

As he put his arm around her, she leaned on his shoulder. She didn't say anything for a long time, but sat sniffling. Garrett prayed for helpful words to say to her. When none came, he just sat and held her for several minutes until she spoke.

"I'm sorry I yelled at you the other night. I'm glad you're my protective brother."

"I'm sorry I got into your business. I just worry about you and want you to be happy."

"I will be. I'm just confused now and don't know what to do."

Just like the last time she said it, he wanted to know what she was confused about but didn't want to upset her again. Since she didn't answer before, he knew to tread carefully.

He gave her another squeeze and kissed the top of her head. "If I can help you, I want to. I don't want to butt in to your business, but I'm here if you want to talk about it."

"I know. I'm glad you're staying."

He let out a long breath. *I'll stay as long as it takes.*

The next morning he woke up early after another dream about Brianna. *Lord, help me to forget her.* He took a short run on the beach, praying with every step for Laci, Brianna, and himself.

He and Laci had talked late into the night about the decisions they had in front of them, and they had come up with a plan of sorts. They decided to go through the house, sorting and clearing out some of the stuff that had gathered there over the years first. Once done with that, they would continue with the fixing-up projects he had started and prepare to put it on the market as soon as they could. Neither wanted to live in the place that stored so many painful memories longer than necessary.

Certain that both Laci and God wanted him to stay, he called the airline and put off his return flight. He resigned himself to staying in town for at least a few months and asked God to help him to avoid Brianna during that time. Spending his time working on the house and trying to help Laci would keep him busy. Even though he didn't have any clue about what was going on with her, she seemed to be at peace knowing he was staying. That was enough for now.

Starting in the attic made the beginning of the sorting process pretty easy. It was bittersweet seeing so many of Mom's things up there, and they reminisced as they filled boxes. Laci fought tears as they filled the trunk of her car.

When he brought out the last suitcase they were donating along with most of Mom's clothes, she broke down. "This feels like saying goodbye to Mom all over again."

He set the suitcase down and gave her a long hug. "I'll take this stuff over, okay? I don't want this to be harder on you than it needs to be."

She shook her head. "I can go. I just need a minute."

When she walked inside to wash her face and get her car keys, he heard a car screeching to a halt behind him.

Brianna slammed her car door and stormed toward him with smoke coming out of her ears. His heart leapt even as he prepared for yet another confrontation.

What did I do this time?

Chapter 40

BRIANNA COULDN'T BELIEVE WHAT she was seeing. It was obvious from the way Laci walked into the house that she was upset. It was easy to guess why, since Garrett was standing there next to a suitcase.

He knows Laci needs him, and he's leaving anyway. What is wrong with him?

I can't believe I was coming here to tell him I loved him. He was going to leave again without a word to me. She fumed as she stormed across the lawn.

"Garrett, what is wrong with you?"

"What are you talking about?"

"She needs you, and you're just going to leave her behind like yesterday's garbage! How could you do that to her?" She cursed the tears that started forming again.

"You don't know what you're talk—"

"You can't just go around leaving people who need you!" She stood inches away from him with her hands on her hips.

The corners of his mouth turned up, and he took a step forward until they were almost nose to nose. "Did you just change the subject again?"

She wanted to slap the flirty smile that was forming right off his face. "You said you would stay for her. You said you were fighting for me." She kicked herself for saying anything about herself.

Hoping he didn't catch what she said, she focused again on Laci. "She needs you, Garrett."

"And what about you?" He stood looking into her eyes and as much as she tried, she couldn't look away.

"We're not talking about me. Your sister needs you. You need to stop leaving people who need you." Her voice sounded shrill, but she couldn't help it. She was too angry and hurt for calm conversation.

"I'm not leaving her." He stepped close enough that they were almost touching, and his breath joined hers. "Now what about you? Do you need me?"

Yes.

No.

It took all of her resolve not to lean into him and beg him to stay.

He reached out and put his arms around her, pulling her against him. "Are you going to keep fighting this?" His voice was low and quiet, and his gaze seared into hers.

She couldn't imagine him leaving again. She couldn't take it and wasn't going to give him an excuse to. "Stay and fight with me. Fight for m—"

He silenced her with the kiss she had missed so much for so long, the one she thought she would never have again. As she threw her arms around his neck, she felt like she was taken back in time, back to when it was safe to love and need and depend on him.

When he broke the kiss to look into her eyes, they both struggled to catch their breath. "Brie, I wasn't leaving. I'll stay here forever if you want me."

"I want you to stay. I need you to stay."

"What about the family dog?"

"The what?"

He raised his hand to about Corey's height. "You know, tall guy, the one you tried to convince me you were in love with the other night."

"I finally stopped trying to convince myself that I was in love with him." She kissed him with everything she had. "You're the only one I could ever love."

"I love you too. And I love it that you still kiss like you mean it." When he grinned at her, her knees almost buckled. Fortunately he was there to hold her up.

"You know I mean it. You got my first kiss and my only kisses, and you'll get my last."

Later that night, they hauled an armful of blankets and a cooler with them to their old favorite spot on the beach. As they lay there holding hands and looking at the stars, Garrett was quiet.

She couldn't help but break the silence. "It's beautiful, isn't it?"

"You have no idea." His voice sounded gruff, as if he was fighting tears.

She turned so that she could look at him. As he reached out and put his arm around her, he kissed her temple. "I've been waiting for years to look at the stars."

"Me too. They're better with you."

"I mean to look at them, period."

She propped herself up on her elbow and searched his eyes that were still focused on the sky. "I don't get it."

He finally looked at her, his eyes glistening in the faint moonlight. "Do you remember what I told you about looking at the stars when we were apart?"

She nodded. "That we could always look at the stars and know we were both under the same sky so we wouldn't feel so far away from each other."

"Right. They kept me sane the first year I was at Michigan and thought you understood what I was doing. I imagined you thinking of me under them like I was thinking of you. When everything fell apart and I knew I wouldn't watch them with you again, I couldn't stand to look at them."

"You didn't look at the stars for all this time?"

"I couldn't without you."

She wrapped her arms around him and looked into his eyes. "I'm sorry I questioned you, Garrett."

"I'm sorry I gave you reason to. I'll never give you another reason to doubt me or let me go."

"Watch the stars with me forever?"

"Forever."

Did you pick up on any marital distance between Quinn and Claire? Read on for a peek as he wakes from his coma!

A Note from the Author

It's somewhat miraculous that this book came to be, because while I was writing it, some huge changes happened in my life. After thinking and praying about moving from metro Detroit to the place in northern Michigan that Summit County is modeled after, I decided to do it. After all, if my fictional characters could move to a beautiful small town up north and start over, why couldn't I?

Within a month of making the decision, I gave notice at work, put my condo on the market, and prepared myself for a new life. During all that upheaval, the fictional world of Summit County was a perfect escape. I will admit that I caught myself looking for the characters on more than one occasion at the farmers market and sidewalk sales after moving :)

Through it all, Brianna and Garrett kept me company. If you've read my notes in other books, you may remember that there have been several characters who started as scene fillers or side characters but ended up having significant roles later. Some—Rachel, Clay, and Faith, for example—even got their own stories. Can you imagine Summit County without them?

Correct answer: Noooo!

Anyway, add Brianna to that list. She was supposed to have a role in Rachel's story and that was going to be it, but one of my beta readers gushed that she couldn't wait to see more of her and went on to extol her virtues as a character. She was right, of course!

If you read my note in Taking Risk, you know I considered matching Brianna with Clay. But as you can see, there was a perfect man for her and he was waiting for his turn to be introduced in Summit County. She needed someone who could match wits with her, be strong enough for her, and be someone who she could have some serious sparks with. Enter Garrett.

I wanted him to have as much disdain for her as she had for him, and it was such fun to write their hatred for each other! (You knew writers were sort of twisted, right?) I loved having her think he was off playing and surfing his life away when he was doing life-saving work on the other side of the world. In the first version of this story, Garrett was Clay and Derek's cousin, but it was just too hard for new readers to follow the family lines and conversations with other family members. I'm still a little bummed that I changed it, but it seemed necessary at the time.

My critique partner, Rose Fresquez, was a great help with some of the details on Garrett's time in Africa. He was originally going to be working in Botswana (simply because I love saying the word), but when she told me she was from Uganda, I changed the country in her honor. She even helped with names and told me about children chanting the word for whites, mzungu, and trying to touch their hair and skin. It was so fun researching for his trek home, and I even made an actual flight itinerary for him. Fun fact: the flight number called in the airport in Chicago is an actual flight to Traverse City. At least it was when I made that itinerary in 2019.

Laci was another one of those characters who took me by surprise. Garrett needed to have a reason to stay in Hideaway, and his scenes with his sister filled my heart. There was no question that she would become a permanent part of the Summit County world. I know you're wondering about her and Zack, so let me assure you that this is not the last you'll see of them—okay, okay. Yes! Of course they'll have their own story soon.

In the meantime, we need to get poor Quinn out of his coma and back into Claire's arms. Did you get the idea that there might be a marital rift there? I tried to only drop a few subtle hints into Brianna and Garrett's story, because the family doesn't have any idea that they've been struggling. When he wakes up from the coma, he doesn't have any idea that they've been struggling either! God can use anything, even amnesia to bring healing to His children. He's so creative!

If you want to be the first to see a sneak peek of new books and hear about sales as well as see pictures from the real place that looks like Summit County, please subscribe to my newsletter by following the instructions for the QR code on the last page of the book! Newsletters aren't for everyone, so if you would just like to be notified of new releases, you can follow me on Amazon or Bookbub and they'll email you.

Thank you for spending your valuable time with my imaginary friends. If you would like to leave a one or two sentence review on Amazon or Bookbub so that other readers can be introduced to this book, I would be so grateful! They are one of the best ways for readers to find new-to-them authors and books. If leaving a review is just too much (I get it ~ they take precious time that could be spent reading!), but you'd like to leave a rating instead, you can do that too! Thanks for reading!

See you in Summit County,

Katherine

Love Remembered in Summit County

If one person doesn't know a marriage ended, did it really happen?

Waking up alone in a hospital room, Quinn has no idea how he got there. When his beloved wife finally arrives, she looks different, even slightly older.

Learning he had amnesia is unsettling, but what disturbs him is the fear on Claire's face every time she walks into his room—and the gut sense that she's hiding something.

Claire has no idea what to expect when Quinn wakes up. She certainly didn't think he would to look at her with eyes full of love and devotion, as if the past few years didn't happen.

Under doctor's orders to allow Quinn to regain his memory on his own, Claire must hide their troubles as she nurses him back to health. Every moment with him chips at the walls protecting her heart.

Can Quinn find out what is being kept from him before he loses everything he cherishes? Can Claire let God protect her heart and risk hope for her marriage?

Will God bring a second chance to two people who once thought they had a love to last a lifetime?

Sneak Peek ~ Love Remembered in Summit County

Chapter 1

Claire's hand shook as she wiped a tear from her cheek. *Please be true.*

"Mrs. Millard?"

"Yes, I'm here . . . I'm sorry, Phil—could you repeat that?" This call seemed as unreal as the one she received a month ago.

"Of course." A smile carried through in the nurse's voice. "He's awake, and he's asking for you."

Thank You, Lord. It's real!

"Thank you." A sob escaped her lips. "I'm on my way. I'll be there as soon as possible."

As if in slow motion, Claire hit *End* on her phone and stared at the blank screen. She wanted to get up, but she was glued to her chair, her body too stunned to move.

Snap out of it, Claire! Quinn is awake!

Her limbs finally sprang into action. She jumped up from the kitchen table, knocking over her chair and almost spilling the half-empty cup of coffee on her morning devotion book. Wesley darted out from under the table, a blur of black and white as he sought refuge on the bookcase in the living room.

"Sorry to scare you, kitty-boy. He's awake!"

Her heart thudded in her ears as she ran to her bedroom to change out of her pajamas and into clothes. She grabbed the nearest sundress from her closet and pulled it over her head, neither noticing nor caring if it was wrinkled. Running back to the kitchen, she shoved her laptop, chargers, phone, and travel mug into her tote bag.

"He's awake! Gotta go!"

He's awake. He's asking for you.

Tears of relief streamed down her face. Throwing everything into the car, she thanked God over and over for giving her the news she'd been begging to hear for a month.

He's awake.

After getting into her car and turning on the ignition, the full reality of her situation hit her. Her thumping heart skidded to a halt.

Wait.

He's asking for me.

What does this mean?

"What do I do now, Lord? Why is he asking for me? As much as I've prayed for him to wake up, I should only feel happy about this and should be breaking land speed records to get to the hospital. I don't know how to move though. I don't know what to do." As horrible as it had been over the past month to see him in that hospital bed, at least she could be with him and take care of him. "What on earth do I say to him?"

She sat with her hands clutching the steering wheel, willing herself to put the car into gear and make the forty-five minute drive from home in Hideaway to the hospital in Traverse City.

"Lord, give me strength. I can't do it without You—and we both know how badly things turned out when I tried."

She sat there for another moment, staring at her white knuckles and trying to get her bearings. In a daze, she watched her next-door neighbor, Mr. Bradley, put red, white, and blue bunting on his porch railing. One would think the Fourth of July parade that was taking place in a few days was going to come down their street by the careful way he decked out his house. She watched him as thoughts of what would be waiting for her when she walked into Quinn's hospital room spun in her head.

Seeing his unconscious body with all the tubes, bandages, and monitoring equipment attached had become normal, as had the sounds and the smells of the intensive care unit. She knew the nurses by name, knew all the doctors' schedules, and knew what the numbers on the machines that surrounded his bed meant. The knowledge she was developing of head injuries and comatose states was approaching encyclopedic, and she had even been prepared to a certain degree for the upcoming stint in rehab and the possible need for him to re-learn to walk and talk.

She was as ready as she could be for what lay ahead for him physically. Still, she was completely unprepared to walk into that room, to look him in the eye.

The charade was about to end.

Chapter 2

Quinn kept his eyes closed and listened to the conversation the two nurses at his bedside were having about him. He hoped that as long as they assumed he was sleeping they would talk enough for him to learn something, but so far they'd only talked about his vital signs and coloring. None of their words were helping him piece together what was going on or why he was so banged up and in what could only be a hospital room.

His head hurt. Breathing hurt. Bones he didn't know existed hurt.

What he couldn't figure out, though, was why he was alone in the hospital room. *Where is Claire?*

His mind had started to veer toward the worst possible answer to his question, but finally one of the nurses gave him the answer he needed.

"Phil got ahold of his wife. She's on her way."

Why wasn't she already there? She must have had to step away just briefly, because there was no way that she would have left his side when he was lying in a hospital bed.

The nurses' conversation before they left the room didn't give him any clues about how he had gotten to what appeared to be an intensive care unit. He tried to remember what had happened, but the last thing he remembered was being with Claire at their new home.

They had been sitting on the deck that Claire's brother, Joe, and Quinn had finished a few hours earlier, looking at the colors of the September sunset. It was a fitting end to a long weekend of working on projects at the home they had moved into two weeks earlier. Joe was an architect, and he had designed the deck and helped Quinn build it with wood that Dad and Mom had given them as a housewarming gift. Claire and her mom, Sue, had cleaned up the garden and planted some shrubbery along the freshly-painted back fence, and it was starting to look like the sanctuary he and Claire had envisioned when they bought the place.

The day was perfect. It was the weekend after Labor Day, and with the temperatures starting to cool down and fall breeze picking up, it was a great work day. The only furniture they had for the deck so far was a rocking bench, and at the end of the day they sat side-by-side, polishing off their lemon custard ice cream from the stand by the grocery store.

Claire's eyes scanned the yard. "I still can't believe this is ours, Q. When we promised each other on our honeymoon that five years from then we would have our student loans paid off and would have a house where we could start our family, even I thought we were a little overconfident."

"Me too. But we did it! Living on Ramen noodles and not having cable was worth it, wasn't it?"

"It's everything I could have hoped for, and all that sacrifice was worth it." She looked back at the modest three-bedroom ranch as if it was the Taj Mahal. "I still can't believe we did it."

"You're right. We're amazing." He put his arm around her and kissed her on the cheek. "You're amazing. I love what you did with the yard."

She smiled as she rested her head on his shoulder. "Thank you, and you were right about putting the burning bush over there for fall color. This deck is definitely my favorite part of the house." Leaning into his embrace, she put her arms around him. "That might just be because you're here though."

"Are you saying I improve a room?"

"You improve everything." She leaned up and kissed the spot on his neck that she had always been partial to nuzzling, then snuggled closer. "So, the question is the same—where do you see us five years from right now?"

"My Claire, always the planner." He smiled and put his hands out toward the yard, forming brackets with his fingers as if setting up a video shot. "I see you sitting right where you are, round and pregnant and absolutely beautiful. And over there . . ." He gestured to the flat corner of the yard. "I see me helping our son and daughter make sandcastles together in the sandbox I built for them."

She stuck her lower lip out in a pouty frown. "Why don't I get to make sandcastles?"

He grinned and winked. "Because you're also holding the baby."

Her blue eyes became as round as saucers as she gasped and laughed. "Three kids and another on the way in five years?"

"We've always said we wanted them close together."

She giggled. "That's true. Hopefully the first one is already in there, and we can get this house filled with noise and smudges on the walls soon."

He leaned over and spoke into her flat belly. "Hey, are you in there, little boy or girl?"

"Okay, let's plan to be here in five years making sandcastles with our three and a half kids." She ran her fingers down his arm as she looked wistfully over at the sandcastle spot. "That's a great spot for a sandbox too. I'll even be able to watch the kids from the kitchen window when I'm washing bottles."

"And I'll wash the bottles while you make sandcastles too." He lowered his voice and leaned closer. "I'll also take the little monsters to their grandparents' houses so we can have some privacy to make more."

As he wiggled his eyebrows at her, she laughed. "It's a deal. We'll need to stay in practice so we can help God fill the house, after all."

"I like the way you think, Mrs. Millard." He took her hand and traced kisses along her fingers.

"You know our parents are going to fight over who gets to babysit, so your job of arranging babysitting should be pretty easy."

"I'll be highly motivated to be alone with you, so even if it's not easy, I'll convince them. I am in sales, after all."

Her blue eyes took on a serious look as she reached up and cupped his cheek. "Promise me we'll always have fun together and be here for each other, even when we have ten kids."

"I promise that too. Nothing could ever change what we have." He stroked her stomach as he mused, "I wonder if our firstborn is in there right now."

"I hope so."

Getting a mischievous look in her eye, she stood and reached her hand back to him.

He frowned. "Hey, where are you going?"

Her eyes twinkled as she bent forward and spoke in the flirty voice that she knew drove him wild. "We're going inside. These babies aren't going to make themselves, you know."

Giggling, she turned and ran into the house. "Catch me if you can!"

He bolted from the bench and chased her inside, catching up to her quickly in the hallway and pulling her into his arms. "I'm always gonna catch you."

"I'm always gonna let you." She wrapped her arms around his neck and pulled him close to whisper in his ear. "Always."

He pinned her to the freshly painted wall and planted a kiss on her that was intended to make her toes curl before lifting her and carrying her to their other favorite part of the house.

Quinn was pulled out of the memory when one of the nurses walked back into the room and adjusted something on one of the machines. Had something happened later that night that he didn't remember? He couldn't imagine what it could have been, but whatever it was broke him into pieces and put half of his body into a cast. It must have happened that night or early the next morning, because that was his most recent memory.

It was strange not to remember an accident, but maybe that was for the best. Claire would surely tell him all the details when she got there. She would make everything okay.

Acknowledgments

God gets extra bonus points for this book. All of the books are covered in prayer, but this one got a lot more airtime than any of the previous stories. Not only was it slightly tricky to incorporate so many previous characters without losing readers who hadn't read anything about Summit County, but writing while also focusing on moving was challenging, to say the least! It was such a blessing to escape to Summit County after long days of packing, throwing away over half of my possessions, and preparing my condo for sale. He stayed with me every step of the way and reminded me what this book was about when I got distracted.

Friends and family are such an amazing gift during all seasons of life, but those days of sorting, packing, storing, hauling and unpacking were a bit crazy. Several friends offered an obscene amount of time and help. One even offered her empty condo during my transition time, and it was the perfect place for quiet evenings with Garrett and Brianna. This book would not have come about if not for the generosity of those amazing people.

My beta readers, critique partner, editors, and proofreaders are always invaluable, but with this book they had to do some heavier lifting—then they gave *me* the heavy lifting! There were some alterations required after a couple of beta readers who had never read any of my books found themselves confused with all of the characters, and they weren't exactly enchanted with Brianna. Not having a history with her, they didn't see the big heart that fans of the series saw. I went back to the drawing board and softened her up, along with changing Garrett's relationship with the Coopers.

I always save my readers for last in this list, because you make this whole thing a blessing I could never have even imagined. Thank you for coming along with me!

About the Author

Katherine Karrol is both a fan and an author of sweet Christian romance stories. Because she does not possess the ability or desire to put a good book down and generally reads them in one sitting, she writes books that can be read in the same way.

Her books are meant to entertain, encourage, and possibly inspire the reader to take chances, trust God, and laugh in the midst of this thing we call life. The people she interacts with in her professional world have absolutely no idea that she writes these books, so by reading this, you agree to keep her secret.

If you would like to talk about your favorite character, share who you were picturing as you were reading, or just chat about books and pretty places, you can email her at KatherineKarrol@gmail.com or follow her on the usual social media outlets. She's most active on Facebook, where she has a small reader group and loves to talk about books. The next most likely place to see evidence of her existence is Pinterest, where she has boards for all of her books, memes, and other bookish things. She seems to think that Instagram is a place to look at other posts but usually forgets to make her own. Maybe someday she'll get on the ball with that. Maybe.

Books

Summit County Series

Second Chance in Summit County

Trusting Again in Summit County

New Beginnings in Summit County

Taking Risk in Summit County

Repairing Hearts in Summit County

Returning Home in Summit County

Love Remembered in Summit County

Surprise Love in Summit County

Playing Married in Summit County

Hearts of Summit Series

Stay for Love

Open the camera app on your phone and aim it here to get a link to join my email community!

If the QR code is too confusing, just email me for the link :)

Made in the USA
Columbia, SC
13 July 2022